S0-ACH-375

"Are we safe?"

"For tonight," Durell said.

"Tonight can be a lifetime for us," she said quietly. "I want to make it so, Sam."

He leaned toward her and folded her in his arms. There was a wild beauty to her that made her look primitive. Her mouth was open, lips glistening. He held her closer and felt her body tremble, pressed tightly against his. Their kiss was slow and searching and hungry. Durell understood all of a sudden that the girl in his arms was more important to him than anything else he had ever known.

Desire mounted, shook them both, became a storm that could not be denied by either of them a moment longer. . . .

Other Fawcett Gold Medal Books in the "Assignment" Series
by Edward S. Aarons:

ASSIGNMENT—ANGELINA
ASSIGNMENT—ANKARA
ASSIGNMENT—BUDAPEST
ASSIGNMENT—BURMA GIRL
ASSIGNMENT—THE CAIRO DANCERS
ASSIGNMENT—CARLOTTA CORTEZ
ASSIGNMENT—CONG HAI KILL
ASSIGNMENT—THE GIRL IN THE GONDOLA
ASSIGNMENT—HELENE
ASSIGNMENT—KARACHI
ASSIGNMENT—LILI LAMARIS
ASSIGNMENT—LOWLANDS
ASSIGNMENT—MADELEINE
ASSIGNMENT—MANCHURIAN DOLL
ASSIGNMENT—MARA TIRANA
ASSIGNMENT—SCHOOL FOR SPIES
ASSIGNMENT—SORRENTO SIREN
ASSIGNMENT—STELLA MARNI
ASSIGNMENT—SUICIDE
ASSIGNMENT—SULU SEA
ASSIGNMENT—TREASON
ASSIGNMENT—ZORAYA

Assignment • • • • •

TO DISASTER

Edward S. Aarons

A FAWCETT GOLD MEDAL BOOK

Fawcett Publications, Inc., Greenwich, Connecticut.
Member of American Book Publishers Council, Inc.

Copyright 1955 by Fawcett Publications, Inc.

All rights reserved, including the right to
reproduce this book or portions thereof.

All characters in this book are fictional and
any resemblance to persons living or dead is
purely coincidental.

Printed in the United States of America

Chapter One . . .

It came to Durell at the K Section of the Central Intelligence Agency this way:

Calvin Jackson Padgett disappeared.

He vanished from his guarded quarters, slipped past the military police on duty, walked through a compound teeming with activity, passing hundreds of men, got beyond the barbed wire, eluded the radar screen, escaped the copter patrol, and vanished.

From Las Tiengas the orders poured out:

Find him.

Get him!

A score, a hundred, a thousand men began to fan out from the desert experimental base, from Las Tiengas, from the whole state of New Mexico, from the entire Southwest.

Find him, stop him, gag him.

If necessary, kill him!

Calvin Padgett, M.S., Maryland born, electronics technician, age twenty-eight, six feet even, weight 155, sandy hair, blue eyes, small scar on right jaw, soft-spoken. Medical history: excellent check-out on physiological examination; psychiatric tests recently disclosed anxiety neurosis, cause unknown. Dangerous. Armed. Rebellious.

Throughout the country, the search was like a subdued electrical vibration, silent, pulsing, grim. One clue, finally: Padgett called his sister in Washington, D.C. There is a record of the long-distance call in the central telephone office at Las Tiengas.

So it came to Sam Durell:

Get to the girl. See if she knows where he is, why he ran. There isn't much time. Five days. If he opens his mouth, it will only take five minutes and all hell will break loose. He knows too much about Cyclops.

And what is Cyclops?

Nothing you need to know, Durell. Get to the sister. Work fast. Find Calvin Padgett!

Chapter Two ...

Durell stood stiff-legged, feet apart, scowling, listening to the silence in the apartment. It was four o'clock in the morning. A light, cool mist was falling over Washington. He had searched the three rooms carefully, but everything was tidy, nothing to show that every inch of space had been examined. Durell was an expert. In the kitchen, Art Greenwald had put a microphone bug under a cupboard shelf; another was pinned under a lamp shade, another under the bed. A touch of Art's humor. What the hell, Durell thought, what is this?

He had been asleep two hours ago. Now this. Callahan was standing on watch in the dark doorway down the street, near the corner. In the apartment basement, Greenwald and O'Meara, headphones clamped to their ears. In the car parked in the next block, Kelly and French.

But the girl was not here.

She had not slept here tonight, but she was coming back. Or was she? Her suitcase stood in the tiny foyer. It had been locked, but Durell had opened it and looked through it and now it was locked again. Deirdre Padgett, ready to travel. Where? When? And why wasn't she here?

He stood still, listening, absorbing, feeling the girl's presence in these rooms. Nice. Delicate perfume. Good clothes, smart styling. A tall girl, pleasant, clean, attractive. Red hair and long-legged (he knew this from his search, the lucite brushes, the neat sheer hose), a fine figure (he knew enough about women's clothing, brassieres, lacy underthings to make a damned good estimate). He felt he knew her intimately. It was part of his job, part of his training. You took nothing for granted, for sometimes death came very suddenly to the careless man.

7

He lit a cigarette, the click of his lighter noisy in the silent room. The misty dawn wind blew the curtains inward, but tomorrow promised to be hot in Washington. Durell was a tall man, in his early thirties, with a thin dark mustache and blue eyes as quick to change temper as the sea. He had a heavy musculature. His work in the past, with the old OSS, had required anonymity, and he knew how to keep silent and live with himself in silence, if he had to. His liaisons with women had been quick and easy, nothing deep. You didn't want anyone worrying about you, to make you overcautious, the surest way to get killed. He had inherited impeccable manners from his grandfather, whose notorious career as a Mississippi gambler had left him with some strange gifts.

The telephone rang and he picked it up quickly. Art Greenwald, in the basement.

"Sam? What gives with this bum?"

"I don't know."

"Hot?"

"Signal red."

"Damn. My wife and I were just about to—"

"Get off the line, Art," Durell said. "I'm waiting."

"Check. Roger. Salaam."

Durell hung up.

His cigarette burned down and he crushed it out in an ash tray and then put the butt in his pocket and wiped the cloisonné clean. Somewhere in the modest apartment house a door banged, an elevator whined. He tensed, listening. No one came to the door.

The street lamps were ringed with iridescent halos. Durell swore softly to himself. He wished he knew more about this one. He felt as if he were groping in the dark. He had never known a tighter security clamp.

The telephone rang again. Joe Masterson, at the bus station.

"Sam? She's spotted."

He blew out air. "Where?"

"Just got off the bus from Prince John, on the Chesapeake. I checked Swayney. Hell, there's a tumbledown ancestral home on the shore. Nobody knew about it, but that's where she's been."

"Damn it. And now?"

"She couldn't find a cab. She's on a bus, heading your way. Give her five, ten minutes."

"Good."

He hung up, relief working in him. Then he called Greenwald again and told him to touch Callahan on the corner, and Kelly and French in the car. Time was suspended afterward, while he waited.

He watched for her from the window, deciding what he could say to make her tell anything she knew about her missing brother. It would have to be played off the cuff. Swayney would have liked to work on this girl. He thought of Burritt Swayney, his immediate superior. Swayney had pale codfish eyes and a pursy mouth and an eternal rutting desire. Damn Swayney. I've been in this game too long, he thought. A spy. I ought to go back to something clean and honest, like Grandpa Jonathan's gambling.

He knew he was only kidding himself.

The girl appeared suddenly from around the dark corner. One moment the street was empty, wide, peaceful, pooled with shadow under the poplar trees. The next, here she comes, almost running, wearing a light tan topper over her shoulders. From the window, Durell watched her walk, almost skipping in her haste, from shadow to shadow on the old brick sidewalk. Long legs, red hair. Right. He glimpsed her face. Good bones, wide eyes shining. Shining with what? He saw her run now. Fear. Fright was in her.

Where in hell was Callahan? Durell looked down from the third-floor window at the empty street, the running girl. A lump of darkness sprawled in the doorway where Callahan had been. What had happened? He had left the window only to answer Masterson's call from the bus station.

Alarm jangled in him when he saw the car. It nosed around the corner silently, tires hissing on the wet asphalt, a big car, dark and powerful, sliding up upon the girl. She turned her head and saw it and a small scream came from her that reached Durell and then she started to run in earnest. Durell saw no more of it. He was already moving. Fast.

The door hit the wall as he flung it open and then he was at the steps, going down with great springing leaps, three at a time, swinging on the newel post at each landing. The lobby was dimly lighted. The glass door was heavy, resisting him with the suction of its pneumatic stops. The cool, damp air of dawn slapped at his face.

The girl had stopped running. She stood trembling on the sidewalk, like a doe caught in a trap, not knowing which way to run. Her tan topper had fallen to the wet bricks and he saw she was wearing a rust-red suit, a gold blouse, comfortable shoes. There was something wild and delicate and stricken about her.

A man jumped from the dark sedan and moved purposefully toward the girl. There was menace in his squat body, the swing of his arms as he reached for her. The girl dodged around him, started running again, saw Durell, halted, thinking he was one of them. The man saw Durell at the same time. His face was a white anonymous wedge in the shadows, his mouth spreading in a tight grin. He swung something at Durell and Durell hit him three times, nape, navel, and kidneys. The man folded forward, then backward, and was on the sidewalk, his neural controls paralyzed. Without pause, Durell caught the girl's arm and flung her to one side. She tripped and stumbled as the shot flared from the driver of the dark sedan. The bullet slammed past Durell's ear. His head rang.

"Callahan!" he yelled. "Art!"

He had his gun out and the driver in the car saw it and slammed the sedan into gear. The car lurched ahead, engine roaring. Durell fired at the rear tire, missed, fired at the gas tank. The car was doing sixty at the corner. It swung in a wide skid, rear wheels spinning, hit the curb, straightened, and was gone.

From around the opposite corner came another car. Kelly and French were in it. Durell waved them on in pursuit of the black sedan. Kelly took the next corner with an identical skid. Durell did not have much hope that they would catch up with their quarry.

He drew a deep breath, turned, and saw that the man he had knocked down on the sidewalk was up again, running with a queer, staggering gait toward the corner where Callahan should have been waiting. And this time Callahan was there, on hands and knees, crawling out of the doorway. The gun glinted in his hand, rapped once, and the running man tripped over his own feet and skidded face down across

the wet bricks and flopped prone, topcoat spread wide, like
a dead bat. Durell swore and ran toward him.

A face that didn't mean anything. A hole through the
side of his head. Dead. Silent. Who he was, what he was,
why he was after the girl—gone.

Ignoring Callahan, Durell swung back to the girl. She had
not moved. She stood pressed against an iron hairpin fence,
the back of her hand to her mouth. Her eyes glinted white
with her terror.

"Miss Padgett?"

She nodded quickly, mutely.

"You're all right. Please stay here. The danger is over."

"You're police?"

"In a way."

He saw that she was not going to run away again, and
this time he crossed the street with a long stride and went
to Callahan. He heard Greenwald and O'Meara come tearing
out the basement door of the girl's apartment building, but
he didn't look back. Callahan was on his feet now, holding
his head. Blood made dark wriggling lines down the side of
his face.

"What happened to you?" Durell asked.

"I don't know. One minute I was standing here, watching, like. The next minute the lights went out."

"Somebody caught you from behind. They were laying
for this girl and they knew we were waiting for her, too.
Who?"

"Christ, who knows?"

"Did you shoot for his head?" Durell asked.

"No. Hell, is he dead, like?"

"Like a mackerel. Forget it. You couldn't help it."

"Sam, I'm sorry."

"Forget it. Check out. Take care of your noggin."

Greenwald and O'Meara were with the girl. Durell waved
them away and took her arm.

"Are you all right, Miss Padgett?"

She nodded, eyes still wide, still frightened. And more.
Her eyes hated him. Durell caught it before her expression
was veiled.

"Let's go upstairs. We've got to talk to you."

"About my brother?" She resisted his hand on her arm.

"Yes. About Calvin Padgett."

"You're all alike, aren't you?" she said bitterly.

"What?"

"Why don't you leave me alone?" she asked.

"I'm sorry," Durell said. "I can't do that."

Chapter Three . . .

Greenwald and O'Meara took care of the man Callahan had shot. Callahan rode away in the ambulance Greenwald called for the anonymous corpse. The street was alive with lighted windows, querulous voices. Two prowl cars calmed things down, and then Durell went upstairs with Deirdre Padgett, back into her apartment. Her shoulders were stiff, resenting him. He wished he knew why.

The apartment was furnished in bright, fresh colors, with a white chunky couch and good, colorful oils on the walls. The girl went in first, snapping on various lamps. Her rust-red suit went well with the place; she made it complete. She gave only a casual glance at her packed suitcase.

Durell looked at her with satisfaction because she was even better than he had thought. There was a quiet, dignified beauty in her clear face, and a strength in the firm shape of her mouth, in the steady way her gray eyes regarded him. Fear washed back into her eyes, and was gone. Resentment took its place again. And hatred. Then nothing at all, a blank, while her mind retreated to some distant place he could not fathom. Yet he liked her immediately.

"You need a drink," he said.

"Please. You probably know where it is by now."

He halted. "Are you accustomed to having us search your place?"

"It happened—once before."

"When?"

"Please. The drink."

He found Scotch and poured it over ice cubes in the kitchen and brought a tumbler back to her. She sat with her long legs crossed, quietly, as if nothing at all had happened outside. Her red hair was shoulder-length, filled with deep

13

coppery highlights. A bracelet of Mexican silver showed on her right wrist. Her purse was of the same golden hue as her blouse, a rich leather, with a big black plastic catch.

He watched her drink. Then he watched her shudder. He made no move to help her or to comfort her. She put the glass down and leaned forward and made a small gasping sound, as if she were going to be sick. He drank his Scotch. It tasted smoky and bitter. His dark-blue eyes studied Deirdre Padgett with quiet interest.

She gasped again. "Damn you."

"Go ahead. Let it up."

"I won't be sick. I *won't!*"

"Who were those men on the street?" he shot at her.

"I don't—" Her head lifted. She hated him. "Oh, you bastard."

He grinned. "That's better. Who were they?"

"I don't know."

"Is that the truth?"

"Yes."

"Never saw them before?"

"Never."

"Why were they trying to snatch you? Or maybe they were trying to kill you. Which?"

"I don't know."

"Which? Or why?"

"I don't know either answer."

He took her glass from her. Her fingers felt cold. He saw the fear crawl over her face and he resented it, as if something wet and ugly were creeping over the petal-fresh skin, the lovely mouth. He sat down across the room from her, looked at the telephone, hoped it wouldn't ring too soon, and lit two cigarettes, got up again, gave her one. Looking down at her, he saw the way her dark lashes made small silken fans against her pale skin. There were tiny freckles across the bridge of her nose that no amount of cosmetics would ever conceal. He liked them.

"This is about your brother, of course," he said quietly. "Frankly, I don't know too much about it, except that he has disappeared and the country is being turned upside down for him. He must be important, but I don't know why. It's twenty-four hours since he vanished from the Las Tiengas Experimental Base. I'm going to find him. You're going to help me."

"No."

"Don't you want us to find Calvin?"

"Whatever he is doing, he must be right about it."

"You're that sure of him?" He was surprised.

She sounded proud. "Cal is my brother. I know him well. He wouldn't do anything wrong."

"Then perhaps he's in trouble and needs help."

"No," she said positively.

He pounced. "Why are you so sure of that?"

She bit her lip. "Oh, you're so clever. You're all so infernally clever."

"He telephoned you here, didn't he? Yesterday evening."

"No."

"There's a record of it, Miss Padgett."

"I don't care."

"You're all packed, ready to go. Are you going to meet him?"

"I won't tell you anything," she said.

He was puzzled. This was a stopper. She looked innocent and clean, fine and sweet, and she sat there hating him and what he stood for. He dragged at his cigarette and it tasted harsh, burning his throat. He listened to the ebbing echoes of sound from the street below.

"Where is he, Miss Padgett?"

"I won't tell you."

"But you know, don't you?"

He saw tears glimmer on the dark lashes. She bit her lip again. Down in the basement, he knew, Greenwald and O'Meara were getting it all down on tape. Not that it would do a fat lot of good. He felt angry and frustrated by the girl's unexpected hostility. Well, what did you expect? Did you think she'd fall all over you and call you Sir Launcelot because you pushed off a couple of thugs down on the street? This girl was tougher than that. There was a hard core in her that would take trouble to reach. Not hardness, really. Pride. Old family tradition, strong fiber, Maryland aristocracy, poor but proud. She worked as a fashion editor for one of the Washington dailies; he had learned that much about her when Swayney routed him out of bed and pushed him into this. He could understand how she felt, loyal to her brother. He knew, all right, suddenly thinking of his grandfather, ninety-five, straight as a steel blade, living on the old hulk of a Mississippi side-wheeler down in Bayou Peche Rouge. Sothron steel. It was hell.

He tried another reach. "Why did you go to Prince John tonight, Miss Padgett? I know your family home is there, but nobody lives there now, do they? Why did you go there tonight?"

"I wanted to."

"Just like that? You wanted to?"

"I often go there."

"But why tonight?"

"No special reason."

"What did you do there, or put there, or take from there?"

"Nothing."

"We can find out, you know. We'll have to search. And time is apparently important. It's important that we find your brother before he talks about his work."

Silence.

And the hating.

He smiled at her, although he wanted to slap her. "What's the matter with me? Two heads? Green hair?"

"You people did enough to Calvin," she said bitterly.

"What?"

"Last year. The Committee. Alleging he was disloyal. It was a terrible ordeal for Calvin. I began hating you then."

"He's that Calvin Padgett?"

"Yes. *That* one."

Damn Swayney, the pursy-mouthed fool. The idiot. Waking him from a sound sleep, no briefing at all. He remembered about Calvin Padgett, and he was surprised to remember Padgett with sympathy. A nice-looking guy, one you warmed to instinctively, the kind you made friends with easily and liked and bought drinks for. Brilliant. Defiant. Denying any membership in the organizations that had his name down there on their rolls in black and white as a member. He was cleared. Judged loyal. A mistake had been made somewhere, but nobody was sure just what. Now he had disappeared. A royal mistake. Gone with some damned secret that could rip the world apart, to judge by the quiet, convulsive, desperate efforts being made to find him before it was too late. He looked at the girl with less warmth.

"So you think your brother was hounded, mistreated, abused?"

"I do."

"He was given his job back, in a highly ticklish, sensitive position."

"Only because the work couldn't have gone on without him!"

"And you feel persecuted by us, too?"

"I don't want to talk about it," she said.

He was angry now. He thought of telling her what it could mean, putting personal pride, spite, petty hatred over the safety of the country. Hell, she would say he was waving the flag. Well, he was willing to wave it. He wanted to keep it waving. But surely she knew all that. There was an innocence in her that he could sense even through his anger. There was something else that kept her mouth shut. He looked for the fear in her eyes. It was still there. She glanced away from him.

"Don't," she murmured.

"It's important. Tell me where he is."

"I can't tell you."

"You can't—or you won't?"

She gave no answer.

"Did somebody warn you to keep quiet? Those men in the car, for instance?"

She shook her head.

"You still don't know who they are or what they want with you?"

"No, no, no."

He sighed.

The telephone rang. Burritt Swayney.

"Anything, Sam?"

"Not yet."

"What in hell?"

"Yeah," Durell said.

"She there with you now?"

"Yes."

"No talkee?"

"No washee."

"There's nothing on the punk Callahan ventilated between the ears. Absolutely nothing. We're working in high gear. FBI files checked negative. No identification on the body. Funny, hey?"

"I'm laughing," Durell said.

"And Kelly and French lost the black sedan."

"I expected that."

"Sam, you've got to find that man."

"Make a song out of it," Durell said, and hung up.

It was full daylight outside, suddenly. When he looked at Deirdre Padgett, he saw that she was crying silently, the tears sliding wet down her cheeks.

Chapter Four . . .

When Durell left the apartment, a new crew took over the watch on the girl. Lew Osbourn was in charge, a gangling, pipe-smoking man with thinning hair and warm, friendly eyes. In Cologne, Lew had once saved Durell's life from a fanatic sniper perched in the skeletal ruins of the town. Lew had a wife, Sidonie, a French girl he had brought home from the wars. And now he had two children, twin girls. They lived in a new development out near Alexandria.

In the lobby of the apartment house, Lew sent his men to various points of vantage and personally took the front hallway himself. He winked at Durell.

"Go on over to the house and Sid will make you breakfast. You look beat, you stupid Cajun."

Durell grinned. "Brioches and hot chocolate?"

"Hell, no. I'm teaching Sid how to cook American style. Buttermilk pancakes and black coffee. I hear the babe upstairs is quite something."

"Look out for rough stuff, Lew. Can I take a rain check?"

"The twins miss you. Especially the candy you bring."

Durell grinned again. "You're a lucky dog."

"Hell, who's stopping you from the same?"

"Maybe if Sid had a sister," Durell said. "See you, Lew."

He went out into the light of the new day, found his car parked under the poplar trees where he had left it at three in the morning, and drove through the winding, early-morning streets of Washington, N.W. It was the first of July, and it was already hot, as he had expected. He felt better for having talked to Lew, after Deirdre Padgett's silent tears.

He had breakfast at a stand on Fourteenth. Stale coffee and doughnuts, left over from the night before. The morning sun made the wet streets steam. At seven o'clock he drove toward Rock Creek Park and 20 Annapolis Street.

The brass plaque on the gray-stone front of the big Georgian house read simply, "The Johnson-Kimball Company," in dignified letters. He felt gritty and tired, his shirt already sticking to his back as he entered. As he went through the Italian marble foyer he heard the busy rattle of office machines in the cover offices that formed a façade for the real business conducted in the building. The elevator man was young and husky. He looked at Durell with photographic eyes and said, "Good morning, Mr. Durell. Hazel's called down twice to see if you showed."

"Thanks, Alex." Durell went up in the elevator to the third floor, passed two doors that looked wooden but that were built of armor-plate steel, and down a long corridor into the adjacent gray-stone house. All the light was artificial, since none of the windows were really windows. When he opened his office door, Hazel looked up and quickly gathered some papers from her desk.

"Hi, Sam. You, too, eh? Nobody got any sleep last night. Swayney is waiting for you."

"Don't fret, Hazel."

He went into his inner office and flicked a finger across the neat stack of personal mail that included an alumni bulletin from Yale, a clothing bill, a rent bill, a letter from a couple he had befriended in England during the war, and a battered, dog-eared envelope postmarked Bayou Peche Rouge and addressed in fine copperplate. He put the last in his pocket and went to the outer office again and Hazel.

"Set up an interview for me with Dickinson McFee, will you, please?"

She looked appalled. "The General? If you top Swayney, he'll pout for a month."

"Can't be helped. I need the information. Set it up, eh?"

On the second floor Durell paused and took a handkerchief and dried his palms meticulously and then walked through a room that contained a battery of electronic computers, through another room where charts and graphs covered the walls, and a Class R administrator was struggling to analyze Middle Eastern reports while teletype bells and phones jangled next door. Swayney's office was beyond all these.

Burritt Swayney, as chief of section, rated a large, airy room with an air-conditioner snoring quietly in a window overlooking a tidy, enclosed garden. Swayney was round and plump and pale, with a habit of making sucking sounds with his small mouth. His eyes were the coldest, palest blue Durell had ever seen. The man was a human memory machine and a confirmed lecher. Durell didn't like him, but for the sake of the work, he got along with him.

"Oh. Sam, hey?" Swayney said. He waved plump hands. "Sit you down."

Durell sat. "I want some facts, Burritt."

"Sure. Sorry there was no time for a thorough briefing. I've got most of the poop. You drop everything else until this is over."

"It's that important?"

"Nothing else matters. Find Calvin Padgett."

"Tell me."

Swayney closed his eyes and recited: "Born in Prince John. Parents, Franklin Padgett, Mary Sprague Lewis. Good stock. Old aristocracy. Lots of money then. Two siblings— John Franklin Padgett, Deirdre Sprague Padgett. When their investments turned sour, father and mother turned on a gas oven and went out on the kitchen floor. The oldest boy, John, was then eleven. He found them. Something happened, nobody knows what—explosion. John's leg injured. Still a cripple. Brilliant man. Physicist. In charge of electronics at Las Tiengas."

"What?" Durell said. "Calvin's brother was there, too?"

"And still there. Why?"

"Nothing," Durell said. "I didn't know about it."

"Not important. John is perfectly sound. What else?"

"Calvin had trouble with the Senate Investigating Committee."

Swayney nodded, his round head loose on his pipe-stem neck. "Somebody used his name to join various subversive organizations. Calvin was cleared, put back to work under his brother. John vouched for him."

"I see. Anything on the girl?"

"Two years younger than Calvin. Goucher graduate. Brilliant in her own way, works on the newspapers here. Had an unhappy love affair, boy killed in Korea. Keeps to herself since then. Passionately devoted to family, keeps the home fires burning. Quite a babe. Well stacked, I hear."

"Stop licking your chops. Anything else on her?"

"Devoted to Calvin. Cool toward John. Understandable. John is much older than Calvin and Deirdre." Swayney's eyes popped wide open, glacial blue. "Why won't the girl talk, hey?"

"I gather she resents the treatment Calvin got last year."

"Doesn't she understand how important this is?"

"I don't know," Durell said.

"Can we *make* her talk?"

Durell shrugged. "Twist her arm. But I don't think it will work."

"What about the men who tried to grab her? She say anything?"

"A blank," Durell said.

"I identified the meat, finally," Swayney said. "A steel worker named Stanislaus Lujec. Immigrant, hard-working type, no record of crime or subversive affiliations. Looked at his hands, figured his occupation, checked Pittsburgh. Neat, hey?"

"Pin a rose on yourself."

Swayney leaned forward. "You sore about something?"

"I'm in the dark. I want to know more about this."

"Wait a minute. Two hoods try to grab the girl. Why? She knows where her brother is, hey? And they want to know, too. They'd like to get Calvin Padgett. It's neck and neck, who gets him first. And maybe he'll spill everything to the newspapers beforehand. If he does, slit your throat, Sam. Hell breaks loose."

"Why?" Durell asked.

"Cyclops."

"I asked you before. What is Cyclops?"

"Something. A gimmick. If the world hears about it, *kaput*. Maybe bombers come over to blow Las Tiengas off the map. It's that hot."

"You said we had five days to find Calvin Padgett," Durell said. "Why five days?"

"Cyclops goes up on the Fourth of July. Symbolic date. You stand corrected. There are only four days left."

Durell said angrily, "He must be somewhere!"

"Everything else is covered. Your job is the sister. Calvin called her, we know that. She knows something, hey? You squeeze it out of her."

"She hates us all," Durell said.

Swayney grinned. "Put some wax on your mustache. Make her talk."

Durell got up and went out.

General Dickinson McFee was dictating a footnote for the minority opinion to be appended to the weekly intelligence estimate being readied for the President's desk, with copies for the intelligence heads of Army, Navy, Air Force, Joint Chiefs, the State Department, the AEC, and the FBI. McFee was a small man, narrow-shouldered, with a bulging intellectual forehead and pale-brown, tired eyes. You forgot how small he was physically after you were with him any length of time. After a moment he seemed to fill the room. He waved Durell to a metal chair while he continued talking into a tape recorder. Durell smoked and waited.

Then McFee said, "Sam, you need some sleep. You can spare two hours, I suppose. Who is with the girl now?"

"Lew Osbourn."

"He's good, but not that good. You'll have to crack her. Sleep, and then go back there. Talk to her. Take an hour or so. If she won't tell, bring her down here."

"All right. But I need something to convince her. I'm not even convinced myself."

"Anything I can do—"

"Am I a good enough security risk to know about Cyclops?" Durell asked bluntly.

McFee got up and shut the office door and then returned to the desk and snapped off two switches placed in the kneehole. Nothing changed in his small, hard face. Durell watched him and smoked his cigarette and waited, and the General said, "Why do you want to know?"

Durell said, "So I can talk sense. If I'm not convinced, I can't convince the girl. I think she's all right. Just mixed up a little. I think she'll do the right thing, if it's put to her correctly."

"She must not be told about Cyclops."

"All right. And me?"

"Aside from the men working under Dr. John Padgett at Las Tiengas, only half a dozen others here in Washington really know about it. Why should you know, too?"

Durell stood up. "I see. Thanks anyway, General."

He got to the door before McFee told him to wait. He sat down again. He felt tense, hungry, and angry. He didn't know why. The girl was in him, in the back of his mind, and he saw again the ugly animal of fear crawling over her face. His throat felt dry and harsh, and he crushed out his cigarette, noting that he had smoked too much this morning. Dickinson McFee tapped on the desk with a pencil.

"Colonel Mike Larabee is chief security man out at the Las Tiengas Base," McFee said. "Both Padgetts were doing a fine job. You know the type of installation it is?" Durell shook his head. McFee went on: "It has top priority on guided missiles. They've worked on all classifications out there in the desert; those machines don't need men, they think for themselves. They carry tactical lightweight A-bombs. And they've experimented with aerodynamic shapes, functions, propulsive mechanisms, long-range guidance. Everything you can think of. But at Las Tiengas they've gone way to hell and gone beyond ballistic missiles like the Corporal or Honest John. They've worked on rockets, turbojets, pulse jets, ram jets; they've aimed for altitude, guidance, accuracy in beam-riders as in the Nike and Viking, distance in the Regulus and Matador. Hell, I don't have to break it down for you, Sam. You know what our space scientists have done, and what the other side can do. Well, Cyclops tops them all."

"In what way?" Durell asked.

"Cyclops does not come down."

"She free-flights in space?"

"Cyclops orbits at one thousand miles up, circling the globe once every ninety minutes. They hope. Target date is the Fourth."

"I didn't think we were up to that yet," Durell said.

"Nobody thinks so. A lot of money went into it. More than for the Manhattan Project, which developed the A-bomb. We've compressed maybe twenty-five, maybe fifty years of research into the last five. Money talks. Organized effort wins. The thing will work."

"And Calvin Padgett knows all about it?"

McFee nodded. "He worked on the brain for Cyclops. It's all in his head. Suppose he tells the newspapers about it? The world will rock. Or suppose the other side gets their hands on him? Hell to pay."

"Why did he run?"

"Nerves," McFee said. "Emotional disturbance. It's not

clear to me, but he broke down somewhere. He was under medical care, but he escaped. Nobody knows how."

"He's a maniac?"

"Hell, no. Psychotic, maybe. Maybe not. Maybe they bought him and he's already across the ocean. Who knows? All we can do is hope it's not so. You know the only clue we've got is his sister. We hope she knows where he's hiding out, and why. Your job is to find that out for us."

Durell stood up. "I appreciate your confidence. I'll get what we need from the girl. She's got the fright bug from somewhere, but I'll try to break it down."

Frowning, Dickinson McFee tapped the pencil against his teeth. "There is one more thing about Cyclops. She's to be the arbiter of peace, according to the top brass. She circles the earth like a Valkyrie, and if I may mix time and place in my speech, she carries a sword of Damocles poised at the throat of any who may be our enemies."

Durell was startled. "Cyclops will be armed?"

"To the hilt. Policy figures there isn't time to build two of them and just use Mark One for test and research. Cyclops goes up with a warhead and all that will be left will be the man with the push button to make her drop. I told you, we covered twenty-five or more years in the last five. There will be a new star in the heavens after the Fourth of July. What's the matter, Sam?"

"I don't know if I like it."

"Nobody likes it. It scares you, eh?"

"Yes," Durell said. "Doesn't it scare you, General?"

McFee grinned for the first time. "My innards have been green ever since I was briefed on it. Welcome to the club, Sam."

"Thanks for nothing." Durell smiled.

"Get some sleep. Then go back to the girl. Find Calvin Padgett."

Durell went out.

Chapter Five . . .

Durell woke at eleven o'clock. He sat up and went into the shower stall and turned the water on full cold. He had slept for less than two hours. His apartment looked comfortable but drab, familiar but empty. He set coffee to perking in the bachelor kitchen, then shaved with care and laced the coffee with rum and drank it while he dressed in a sober blue suit and a white shirt with a buttondown collar and a plain dark burgundy necktie, loosely knotted. He emptied his gun, a short-barreled .38 Special, cleaned it, reloaded it, and put it under his arm in the pocket specially tailored to hold it without bulging too much.

The apartment depressed him, and this was surprising, for he had always felt all right in it before. Perhaps he should have taken Lew Osbourn up on his offer of breakfast. He enjoyed being with Sidonie and the twins. He felt more at home there than in this place, which merely served as a peg on which to hang his hat. Now wait a minute, he thought. Why all this restlessness? He was thinking of the girl, Deirdre Padgett. The long legs, the smart rust-red suit, the red hair with dark-copper highlights. The low, controlled voice, the wide gray eyes, the—

Forget it.

But maybe Lew Osbourn was right. You can't live alone forever, just because you hate the thought of leaving a widow behind you someday. Or having someone constantly worrying about you. Look at Lew. Doing fine. Sidonie and the twins. Happy as larks. You visit there and you feel the warmth, the friendship, the closed circle of a fine little family.

No.

Anyway, why put Deirdre Padgett in the picture? She

hates you. She resents you. To her, you're a symbol of
everything unhappy that came to her beloved brother. She
doesn't know you exist as a man.

Durell went out of the apartment, his anger spurting in
all directions.

He retrieved his car from a parking lot and drove east
out of Washington, hit Route 5, turned south, took an asphalt side road, and came to Prince John, on the Chesapeake.
It was noon by then. The sun was blazing, a hot weight on
the back of his neck. The bay sparkled in a wide expanse of
blue. The Padgett estate consisted of a stone gatehouse and
a big colonial house of faded rose brick, with black shutters
and twin chimneys and a wide sloping lawn that reached
down to the shore. The main house was only an empty shell,
with nothing behind its lovely façade except the wreckage
of a fine Maryland family.

The gatehouse was in better condition. The neat flower
garden and trimmed lawn made an oasis in the wilderness
of rank weeds and underbrush that assaulted the manor
house. Far out on the Chesapeake he traced the smudge of
smoke from an oil tanker plodding south from Baltimore,
bow riding high and empty. Two cars were parked in front
of the gatehouse. As Durell stepped from his coupé, feeling
the sun smite him, he saw Frank Gresham come out of
the house, look at him, and walk over to the picket fence.

"Hi, Sam. Something?"

"Just looking."

"Nothing here. I thought you were working on the girl."

"I am. I just thought I'd drive out for a look."

"Well, the place is clean. We covered it like a blanket. If
she got a message from Brother Calvin, it's in her noodle,
no place else." Gresham looked at him curiously. "Something
biting you, Sam?"

"No."

"Harrison found the black sedan. Stolen, of course.
Wrecked down in Virginia, near Richmond. Burned. So no
prints or anything. I'd say it was burned deliberately to
wipe 'em out."

Durell wondered why he had come here. There was nothing to be learned in this place. He looked up at the hot
sun, feeling its weight, sweating. What was he looking for?
Something about the girl, Deirdre. He wanted to know more
about her, more than he had learned from Swayney's in-

human memory files. Why had she come here last night?
There had to be a reason.

"Did the girl sleep here, do you know?" he asked.

Gresham shrugged. "If she did, she made the bed before
she left."

"Have you checked the local telephone company?"

"Why?"

"I'll do it," Durell said.

"Hell, I never thought of—"

"I just thought of it, myself," Durell said. "See you."

He went to the railroad station in Prince John first. The
tiny town boasted only two cabs, and he spoke to both
drivers, showing his CIA card. They were impressed. One of
them had driven Deirdre Padgett to her house here at eleven
o'clock last night. Was she alone? The driver was incensed,
suspecting a slur upon the flower of Maryland womanhood.
Of course she was alone.

He went to the local telephone office next and spoke to the
manager, a gray-haired, lanky man with an Eastern Shore
drawl. The phone in the gatehouse was still connected, the
bills paid for by Deirdre Padgett. The manager had to wake
up the night switchboard operator, and that took a little time.
When Durell asked his question, he struck pay dirt.

Yes, the operator remembered a long-distance call last
night to the Padgett place. Right spang at midnight.

"Where did the call originate?" Durell asked.

"New Mexico, someplace. Funny name."

"Las Tiengas?"

"Yes. That's it."

"At midnight?"

"Said so, didn't I? Right spang on the dot."

"Who called Miss Padgett, do you know?"

Flush of insult. "I didn't listen. I never listen to—"

"I wish you had," Durell said.

"Well, I didn't."

He was reasonably sure that the girl had come out here
only to receive a prearranged telephone message from her
missing brother. That placed Calvin Padgett still in Las
Tiengas at midnight, twelve hours ago.

It was something. Not much, but something.

He got back into his car and returned to Washington.

Chapter Six . . .

The street was quiet, stifled under the pall of humid heat that had settled over the city. Durell nodded to the agent in the lobby of the apartment house and went up in the self-service elevator to the third floor. The corridor was empty. Lew Osbourn was not in sight.

Frowning, Durell walked first to the open window that overlooked the back courtyard. There was not much he could see through the thick foliage of the poplar trees. Somewhere a baby cried. A radio droned out the thick inflections of a soap opera. Peaceful. Hot. Where in hell was Lew? Durell turned and walked back to the door of Deirdre Padgett's apartment.

Nothing came through to him from inside. No sound, no movement. Worry began to gnaw at him. His mind jumped over the points of the stake-out—the man in the lobby, another across the street, one on the roof, Lew here in the hallway. The girl was in a bottle, the bottle was corked. She couldn't get out, nobody could get in. Not without Lew's permission. Yet he had the feeling that something had happened.

When he tried the apartment door, he found it unlocked, but it opened inward only an inch or two before it met some obstacle behind it. He pushed harder at once, and at the same instant he heard a sudden scratching movement from inside. Alarm jangled. He put his shoulder against the panel and shoved hard. Somebody breathed, quickly, sharply. The shades inside were drawn, and the room beyond the foyer was in cool shadow. Movement flashed beyond the arched doorway, a blur of rust-red. It was Deirdre Padgett.

On the floor beyond the door was a man's sprawled body, blocking his way. Lew Osbourn. Durell looked at the dead

29

man and then at the girl in shocked disbelief. The girl had
Lew's gun in her hand and the gun pointed at him. Her face
was white. Her mouth shook.

"Shut—shut the door," she whispered. "Be quiet."

He leaned back against the door and heard the latch click.
His hand moved toward his inside pocket.

"Don't," the girl said.

He stood motionless.

"I didn't do it," she said.

He stood silent.

"Believe me," she said.

He stood waiting.

Her mouth shook again. There was a small rip in the
shoulder of her suit. There were violet shadows under her
eyes. Fear crawled over her, slimy and ugly. It was quiet in
the apartment. The sun glared in long slivers of brilliance
through the slats of the Venetian blinds.

"Give me the gun," he said.

She shook her head, red hair swinging. "No. No, I can't
trust you."

"I'm going to take it from you," he said. "Go on, shoot."

He walked toward her. Her mouth was partly open. Her
white teeth gleamed. The gun shook in her hand and he saw
her knuckles go tight. He thought she was going to squeeze
the trigger. At the last moment she dropped the gun and it
bounced on the floor, clattering, as he grabbed at her wrist
and twisted it hard. She gave a small, stifled scream. He
threw her angrily aside, without mercy, away from him. She
fell into the couch across the room. Her red hair swept across
her face.

"Stay there," he said. He didn't recognize the sound of
his own voice as he picked up Lew Osbourn's gun.

Lew Osbourn. The knife in his back. Not a gun, a knife.
He saw it now, looking at the dead man from this angle.
A switchblade, buried between the shoulders, not too far below the neck. Into the spinal cord. How far wrong could
a guy get? Thinking of Sidonie Osbourn, the laughing twins,
the little house in the development near Alexandria, he
felt a taste of acid in the back of his throat. His stomach
lurched and heaved. He swallowed. Thinking of Lew, with
more hair in other years, in Cologne, reckless and laughing then, tough, eager to do the job right; but always check-

ing, always alert. How could this have happened, so easily, so silently, so finally?

He felt hate and anger, remorse and pity. He felt a deep, irrevocable dedication to finding the man whose hand had done this thing.

His thoughts jumped back to the girl. Not her hand? But her fault. Because of misguided loyalty, a misguided sense of family duty. That's why Lew Osbourn was dead.

He looked at the apartment again. It had been neat and tidy before. Now he saw for the first time the quick, insane wreckage of it.

"All right," he said to Deirdre Padgett. "Tell me. Make it quick."

"There was a man in here. He came in—"

"How?"

She gestured. "The kitchen window. The fire escape."

He went to the kitchen door. The window over the sink was open. Red-painted iron stairs laddered up into hot sunlight to the roof. But Lew had left someone up there on watch.

"And?" he asked.

"He took me by surprise," the girl whispered. She rubbed her cheek, touched the rip in her suit. "He forced me to be silent. He had the knife. He began to search the place."

"Who was he?"

"I don't know."

"You never saw him before?"

"Never."

"Then?"

"I made a sound. I wanted help. And your friend—this man—came in. I tried to warn him. I don't know what happened. I think the man—the stranger—hit me. I don't remember. I just woke up, a few moments before you came in."

"Did this stranger speak to you at all?"

She nodded.

"What did he want?"

"My brother," she said. "He wanted to know where to find Calvin. But I didn't tell him."

"You're going to tell me," Durell said quietly.

She looked up at him, something sharp on her tongue, gray eyes angry for an instant, resenting him. Then her shoulders sagged. She nodded. She whispered, "I need help. I didn't expect any of this. I'm sorry."

"Come with me," Durell said.

He had made a decision.

She did not object when he told her to climb out onto the fire-escape platform beyond the kitchen sink, nor did she accept his help. Her movements were lithe and graceful. On the steel slats of the platform, she waited for him. Durell looked down at the back garden, but there was little to be seen. The foliage of the poplar trees made an effective screen, and the man on watch at the green-painted back gate was definitely cut off from view. The girl's eyes regarded him gravely.

"Up," he said.

He followed her to the roof, automatically noting the smooth limber movement of her hips, the length of her long, firm legs. The sun made a griddle of the tar-and-gravel rooftop. She paused again, and this time Durell went ahead, toward the housing of the elevator shaft at the far side. He found Tom Elderman there, in the sharp angle of shadow cast by the small structure. Elderman had been Lew Osbourn's working teammate. The agent was unconscious, with a nasty-looking wound on the back of his head, with blood covering one side of his narrow face. Durell felt for his pulse. It was steady enough. Elderman already showed signs of reviving.

He signaled to the girl to join him. Her face was white and her mouth shook again. But her voice was low and controlled.

"Do you believe me now? I didn't kill anybody."

He didn't think she had. Not now. He said, "Deirdre, you're in trouble. Bad trouble. None of this would have happened if you had trusted me before."

She whispered, "I don't know."

"Are you ready to tell me about Calvin now?"

"I—I can't decide."

"You and Calvin are mixed up in something much bigger than you think. Something big and dangerous. You know that now. You know I want to help you. You know that, don't you?"

Her eyes were level in the hot sunlight, studying him. "Yes. I think so. But I won't be bullied. Not even now. I've got to help Calvin, too. If you arrest me, I won't tell anything."

"But surely you can't—"

"I'm sorry. Calvin comes first."

"There is a fine man downstairs, and he's dead. Because

of you. Because of this thing you've got about cops, about
me—"

"Not about you," she said quickly.

"All right, then. Where is your brother?"

She was silent.

"Is he in trouble?"

She nodded. "He wants to see me and talk to me before
he makes his decision about something. That's all I can
tell you. I wouldn't even tell you that, but I've got to trust
somebody. I can't—I guess I can't do any good for Calvin
alone."

"Suppose I help you?" Durell offered. "Then will you tell
me what I need to know?"

She bit her lip. "Yes. But how can you? There's been a
murder. You've got to arrest me."

"Come on," Durell said.

She didn't understand. Her face closed against him,
guarded, defensive. He said quickly, "Wait a minute. Look. If
I help you get away from here, if I hold off the arrest, will
you tell me where to find your brother? Or will you let me
go with you? Just me. I promise you, no tricks. Just you and
me, and we'll go to see your brother and talk all this out."

She regarded him with deep suspicion. "If this is a trick—"

"I told you, no trick," he said. "You'll never make it alone,
you know that now. They'll stop you, whoever they are. Or
we will. And then you won't be able to help Calvin at all.
He'll lose out, either way."

"I have no choice, have I?"

He shook his head. "It's not like that. I'm offering you a
deal. I give you my word. I'll help you get to your brother.
But I've got to go with you. Nobody else. Will you trust me
that far? When we see your brother, we'll both know better
what to do next. You'll never get to him otherwise," he said
again. "Surely you can see that."

"But suppose I—suppose I double-cross you? You're taking
a big chance with your job, with everything."

He smiled tightly. "It's I who have to trust you on that."

"You're so very sure of yourself. You're so strong. . . ."

"Come on," he said.

"I won't promise anything."

"All right. We'll let it go at that."

Nobody saw them and nobody stopped them as they made
their way downstairs in the adjacent apartment house and

reached the street. There was no alarm from inside Deirdre Padgett's building. Knowing the way the stake-out was disposed, Durell led the girl to the next corner, waited until several cars crossing the intersection offered them a temporary screen, and went up the next street. Two blocks away he found a combination bar and restaurant. It was cool, air-conditioned, and dark inside. Durell found a booth in the rear and ordered a rum and Coke for the girl and Scotch over ice for himself. It was well after one o'clock.

"Tell me about the man who killed Lew Osbourn," he said bluntly. "Don't omit anything."

She spoke slowly. "I didn't hear him come in. I was taken by surprise. I was sitting there, knowing I couldn't leave the apartment without being followed, wondering what I could do next. Before I knew it, he was there, his hand over my mouth."

"What did he look like?"

She shuddered. "He was big. Ugly and big. He wore a yellow sport shirt and gray slacks. He was a man of about forty, but enormous. And very strong. He looked clumsy, but he moved like a cat, with absolutely no sound."

"Did he speak to you?"

"Oh, yes. He asked me where Calvin was. I didn't tell him, even though he—"

Durell said quickly, "All right. Why did he search your apartment? What was he looking for?"

"He had the knife in his hand. He made me sit absolutely still while he looked around. He was wild, but awfully fast. He thought I had a letter from Calvin, or something. I don't know."

"You'd recognize him again?"

Her mouth moved. "I'll never forget him."

"Did he say anything at all that might be useful?"

She hesitated.

"Go on," he urged. "You must tell me."

"He said something about Calvin, as if Calvin had double-crossed somebody. A man named Gustl Weederman."

Durell frowned. "Do you know that name?"

"I never heard of it before. The man—the killer, I mean —seemed angry when he let the name slip. I think he assumed I knew about it, and then he saw that he had made a mistake, because I obviously knew nothing about it. He kept insisting afterward that I must know about this so-called

double cross Calvin pulled on Weederman. It was as if he
was trying to convince himself. And because he was so
angry, he was a bit careless, and that's when I tried to get
away, through the door."

"And Lew Osbourn then heard you?"

"Yes. He came in so fast—it happened so quickly—"

The waiter came with their drinks. The girl took hers in
both hands, shivering, and the waiter looked at her curiously,
then at Durell. Durell stared at him and he went away. The
girl was breathing in great, shuddering gasps. Her face was
white. There were tiny beads of perspiration on her upper
lip. She whispered, "This time I think I'm really going to be
sick."

He helped her up and led her to the door marked "Ladies."
She went through quickly. Durell looked around the bar and
found a phone booth where he could watch the door through
which Deirdre had gone. He went over to the phone and
dropped a coin in the slot and dialed an emergency number. He got through to Burritt Swayney almost at once.

"Burritt, this is Durell. I've got the girl. I need some dope.
Have you ever heard of a man named Gustl or Gustav
Weederman?"

"What are you talking about? What about the girl?"

"Come on," Durell said urgently. "Use the memory."

"Weederman. Gustav Franz. Last heard from in Vienna.
Naturalized American, suspected of Nazi sympathies during *that* war, worked for the military government in Vienna
in '45. Age thirty-nine, graduate of Leipzig. Family of petty
Austrian nobility. A count, I think. Single. Fired from the
military government on suspicion of espionage for the Rus-
sians. Went through the Iron Curtain." Swayney laughed.
"They executed him."

"The hell they did."

"What?"

"He's over here. Hunting for Calvin Padgett. It's his action
apparatus that's onto the girl. Maybe onto Padgett, too."

"Sam, what happened, hey?"

Durell told him. It was difficult to talk about Lew Osbourn's
death. He finished: "The girl is with me now. I think she
trusts me. If I bring her in, though, she won't talk. She's in a
state of half shock now, I think. She wants to protect her
brother at all costs, so I made a deal. She'll take me to him,
but nobody else. It's a funny thing."

Swayney said sharply, "Bring her in. Don't waste time fooling around."

Durell said, "I want to play it this way. For Lew. Do you understand?"

"Damn you, are you crazy? Bring her in!"

"I tell you, she'll freeze. She won't talk any other way."

"Leave that to me. If her brother's been palling around with Weederman, he's a traitor, he's selling us out. And the girl is just as bad. You can't take that chance."

"You're condemning her already," Durell said. "I'll call back later."

He hung up. Immediately afterward, he called another number that connected him with Hazel, in his office. He told Hazel everything that had happened.

"Will you call Sidonie Osbourn for me?" Durell asked. "I hate to stick you with it, but I may not have time. Tell her I'll be out to see her as soon as I can."

"Of course." Then: "Sam, was that you who just called Swayney?"

"Yes. Why?"

"The whole place is in an uproar. What are you doing?"

Durell said, "My grandfather was a gambler, the best there ever was. I'm gambling on the girl. I think she's innocent, but confused. I think she trusts me a little. I hope so. It's a one-shot throw of the dice."

"Sam, you always said gambling could never be part of this work."

"Call Sidonie, please," he said. Then he hung up.

He was sweating, but he felt cold. He dried his hands on a handkerchief. He wished he could have gone to see Sidonie Osbourn himself. When Deirdre came out of the ladies' room, he moved forward quickly to take her arm and guide her out to the sidewalk, where he hailed a cab. The girl was silent, docile enough now. Her face was pale, but her eyes looked better. Sitting beside her, he could sense the delicate perfume she used. Her mouth looked haunted. It was a lovely mouth, a beautiful face. She was shivering slightly, but he moved away from her on the back seat of the cab so as not to be in physical contact with her. Don't be a fool, he thought. Think of Lew, the two kids. Think of Sidonie tonight. You travel farthest and longest when you're alone. Especially in this business. Any crazy notions you began to have this morning—well, forget them. Drop it, quick. You were right and Lew was wrong; you're alive and Lew is dead. Drop it. Forget it.

He gave the cab driver the address of his apartment.

Chapter Seven . . .

He made a Creole omelet and a fresh pot of coffee in his kitchen and they ate on trays in the living room. The telephone rang twice, but he did not answer it. He did not think Swayney would outguess him and come doubling back to look for him with the girl here. Swayney would look everywhere else first. They had an hour, perhaps, before it became too dangerous to stay.

The girl was silent until they had their coffee. Then she said bluntly, "You called your office from that bar, didn't you?"

He didn't lie to her. "Yes."

"But you still want me to trust you?"

"My orders were to bring you in. This Weederman that you mentioned is a Russian agent. He was supposed to have been executed a few years ago, but apparently it was a phony. He has a smart, tough, and desperate apparatus in operation, determined to get their hands on your brother. Maybe to kill him, maybe to spirit him out of the country. The office thinks Calvin, with his past record, isn't too clean on it. They daub you with the same brush."

"I see," she whispered.

"I told them that I didn't believe either count," Durell said.

"Why not? You don't know anything about me."

He didn't quite know how to answer. "Call it instinct. Call it a gambler's hunch. I think you're innocent."

"Thank you," she said, but he was not sure if her inflection was meant to convey irony or not. "I appreciate your trust in me."

"Look, Deirdre. Two men have already died. One of them

was a member of Weederman's outfit. The other, this morning, was my best friend."

"I'm sorry," she whispered.

"Can you imagine how I feel about it, then? I'm taking a chance, holding you out of the office. You've got to tell me about your brother."

"Yes," she whispered. "I'll tell you what I know. But it won't help you. It will only be of help if you permit me to go to meet him."

"I'll go with you," Durell said. "Then we'll see."

She nodded. "There isn't much time. Four days. No, less. Most of today is gone."

"Tell me about it," Durell said.

She spoke earnestly, her eyes locked with his, waiting for a challenge from him. He listened in patient silence.

"First of all, Calvin is innocent of any treason. He is sensitive, brilliant, a wonderful man. I love my brother, Mr. Durell. He suffered terribly when those unfair charges of treason and dubious loyalty were thrown at him last year. He wanted to quit the work he was doing, but John and I persuaded him to go on with it, because it was necessary and vital to the country, whatever he may have suffered personally. You know about my older brother, John?"

Durell nodded. "Yes."

"Calvin is not a traitor. He told me he had never joined any of the organizations that had his name on their membership rolls. He did not know how they had managed to do that to him. He was able to prove he could not possibly have attended the meetings they said he did. Perhaps it was a plot to discredit him and make him useless to our country. Is that possible?"

"Maybe," Durell said.

"John watched over him very carefully in Las Tiengas. I don't know what they're building out there. I don't want to know. I know it's big and important, that's all. A month ago, John wrote to me that he was worried about Calvin. He wrote that Calvin was getting too moody and introspective, doubting the wisdom of what he was doing—whatever his job required him to do. Last week John telephoned to me. He told me that Calvin had been caught in Las Tiengas, away from the base, against every expressed security order. He told me that Calvin was being held at the base hospital for observation. It seemed utterly incredible to me. I couldn't believe it.

You have to know Cal—he's brilliant, a scientist dedicated to his work, but he's full of fun, too, wonderful to be with, a good companion, levelheaded. John said that Cal had cracked up.

"I didn't hear any more about it until yesterday afternoon, when Calvin called me. He told me he had escaped from the base and that he was alone and deeply disturbed and didn't know what to do. I couldn't make much sense out of it. He said he had to see me, to talk something over with me before he decided on a course of action. He talked about his conscience, about doing the right thing. It frightened me. It upset me terribly. And then he rang off, after arranging to phone me again at the old house in Prince John."

"Did he sound rational then?"

"The second time, yes," she said. "He was very deliberate. He said he would not make the decision without seeing me first."

"Why are you so important to him?" Durell asked.

"I don't know. I suppose he—he must feel confused. We were always very close, in many ways. He would trust me, I think, to see through whatever is confusing him and help him to do what is right."

Durell frowned. "I still don't understand it."

"Well, I said I would go to meet him, wherever he was. He told me to be careful. He said you people would try to stop me and trip me up and question me. He begged me not to tell you anything at all until I came out there."

Durell said, "And where are you to meet him?"

"In Las Tiengas," she said quietly.

"He's waiting there for you now?"

"He said so. Yes."

"Where, exactly?"

She looked at him, hesitating. "If I tell you, what will you do?"

"You must trust me."

"Will you go there with me?"

"Yes," Durell said.

"Alone? Just the two of us?"

"Yes," he said again.

She drew a deep breath. "He said I was to check in at a place called the Salamander, in Las Tiengas. It's a hotel, or a motel, I'm not sure which. He said he would see me there tomorrow evening."

Durell stood up. Instantly alarm flickered across the girl's features. He smiled. "Let's get started."

"Like this? Just as we are?"

He nodded. "Let's go."

She arose, an odd reluctance in her now. "I suppose you think I'm contemptible for not talking to you before. Believe me, I had no idea anyone would be killed. What I did was for Calvin's good, and I'm convinced that whatever he's done, it must be right and honorable. Calvin is not a traitor. He would never give away any vital national secrets."

"Not even to Weederman?"

She flushed. "I told you, Calvin's loyalty is beyond any suspicion. Truly."

"Those men have ways of getting information. It doesn't matter how strong you are, Deirdre. Everybody has a breaking point. Are you sure you want to keep me to this bargain, for just the two of us?"

"If I'm not there, Cal won't show up," she said. "If you send men out there to trap him, he'll know about it, somehow. He's being very wary. Please don't go back on your word. I trusted you."

He smiled. "We're on our way. Just the two of us."

Then the doorbell rang.

Durell heard the girl suck in her breath as the shrill alarm jangled away. Her face paled. She jerked her arm from his grip and retreated from the door. Her eyes blazed with anger and contempt. "You lied to me! You told your men to come here."

"No," Durell said. "Wait."

The bell rang again, enormously loud in the small apartment. The girl backed into the kitchen. There was a rear door that led to a service stairway in the back of the apartment building. Across the street was an arm of Rock Creek Park. Durell started for the door, then spun quickly to restrain the girl. She twisted away, yanked the rear door open, and darted through. Durell plunged after her.

Too late, he saw he had been trapped.

Two men back here on the dark service landing, one holding the girl, a hand clapped over her mouth as she struggled in his grip. Her eyes were wide with terror. And another man, enormous, ugly, in a yellow sport shirt and gray slacks, hair cropped short to the shape of a bullet head hunched on meaty shoulders.

Something swung in the air before Durell could turn or recover his balance. An instant's glittering arc, then a blast of white pain exploded in him and he was on his hands and knees, shaking his head, trying for the gun in his pocket. A heavy shoe slogged into his ribs. He sprawled on his face. He still tried for the gun. The shoe came grinding down on his hand.

"Take the girl away."

"What about *him?*"

"I'll take care of this one. Beat it!"

Durell got half erect in time to see the knee lifting for his jaw, and above it the grinning face of the bullet-headed giant.

Then there was nothing at all for him except a long, deep dive into blackness that screamed momentarily of agonizing pain and became emptiness. . . .

Chapter Eight . . .

He swam sluggishly upward through a sea of red torment, toward the glare of light that opened above him like the mouth of a cone. The doctor working on him was quick, deft, impersonal, smelling of disinfectant. Tape on his ribs, professional fingers on his face, and a bobbing nod.

"Nothing serious or permanent. Hurts like hell, eh?"

Swayney's moon face loomed above him.

"Sam, what happened to the girl? How come you let her get away, hey?" Blue eyes glittered icily. "I gave you firm orders to bring her in and you—"

"Go to hell," Durell said.

A red wave moved over Swayney's face. "Hey? What's the matter with you? Lew is dead, the girl is gone, you were ranting about a dead man named Weederman—"

"He's not dead," Durell said.

"I say he is. I've got all the facts. I'm not usually wrong."

"This time you're wrong."

"Well, what about the girl? Where is she?"

"Gone. Weederman's apparatus got her."

"Oh, Jesus."

"My mistake."

"Your scalp, you mean." Swayney drew a deep breath. "All right. Drop it. You're off it. You go to the hospital, then we'll have this out. Just answer one thing. What made you take off with the girl alone like that?"

"A hunch. A gamble. I lost."

"Did she tell you anything?"

"Some."

"She's a filthy Red bitch like the rest of them. What did she do, show you a leg, Sam?"

"You bastard," Durell said.

"You think I don't have a right to get sore about this?"

Durell said, "The girl received enough of the kind of treatment you want to give her. She took it for her brother and she got enough of it for herself. All right, it wasn't anybody's fault, but she doesn't see it that way. She feels antagonism, she feels she won't get justice for herself or her brother. She doesn't like the idea of Calvin Padgett being hunted down like a bubonic rat. You try your loudmouthed, bullying tactics on her, and she'd clam up. She's tough. You wouldn't get anywhere. So I tried to win her confidence. I did, too. But Weederman's men booby-trapped me."

Swayney's pursy mouth closed as if tightened with a drawstring. Durell pushed the doctor away and sat up. His head swam. Pain hammered at him. He closed his eyes, hearing Swayney's thin voice go on and on. After a moment he felt better, the pain ebbed, he stood up. The man with the bullet head loomed in the back of his mind. Ugly, jeering, deadly. The man who had killed Lew Osbourn. The man who had Deirdre Padgett. He felt sick. He drew a deep breath and steadied himself. Swayney watched him with curiosity.

"You belong in a hospital, Sam," Swayney said, more softly. "I'm sorry, but I'm pulling the cork on you. You're off the case."

"No."

"What did the girl tell you about Calvin Padgett?"

"She is to meet him in Las Tiengas tomorrow evening."

"Where?"

"A place called the Salamander." Durell wanted to hold this out, but he couldn't. Everything he had been trained to be required that he transfer this information, now that the girl was gone. "Cal Padgett is playing it cagey. He won't show unless his sister is there. And I've lost her. If you throw a stake-out on the place, you'll lose, Burritt."

"We'll see who loses."

"I've got to find that girl," Durell said.

"Hell. We've got to find Calvin Padgett."

Dickinson McFee lit his pipe very carefully, puffing hard, watching the flame shoot up and die away as he blew on the wooden match. It was three o'clock in the afternoon. Durell sat patiently in his office at 20 Annapolis Street. His head ached, his ribs ached, his teeth were sore. There was anger in him and a sense of tension he could not dispel. As usual, the

little general seated behind his smooth, cleared desk wore
civilian clothes, a gray flannel suit with a blue necktie and a
pearl stickpin. As usual, Dickinson McFee seemed to fill the
room with his presence. He spoke quietly.

"Swayney is down on you, Sam. With some reason, you
must admit. Don't interrupt me, now. You ought to be in bed
for the next twenty-four hours; but if you say you're all right,
then I'll accept that. Officially, you're off the case. I've got to
back up Swayney."

Durell waited.

The pipe emitted great clouds of aromatic smoke.

"I know Lew Osbourn was your friend," McFee said.

"My best friend."

"You don't want to quit on this one, do you?"

"No," Durell said.

"I'll tell you what I've been thinking. Swayney is throwing
nets out in all directions to snare the girl. I don't think he'll
find her or the son-of-a-bitch who clobbered you and killed
Lew. The apparatus we're working against seems to be smart,
fast, and highly organized. They must not be allowed to get
their hands on Calvin Padgett. The FBI is rounding up every
suspected agent in the country, but it's my hunch that this
crowd is all new, never used before, held in reserve for just
this kind of thing. Swayney won't find the girl. Not alive,
anyway."

"You can't let them kill her," Durell said tightly.

"We'll try to stop it. Swayney is competent on that end.
But it's my hunch she'll crack. She'll have to. It's only a matter
of time, maybe hours, with luck maybe a day, before she
tells about her rendezvous with her brother."

"So?"

"We'll work this on two levels. Swayney is the obvious, the
overt activity that they'll see. He'll throw weight around, here
in the East, and in Las Tiengas, too. The enemy apparatus will
spot it all, you can count on it."

"And the other level?"

McFee pointed the stem of his pipe. "That's you."

Durell felt a great wave of relief wash through him.

"Officially," McFee said, "you'll be in the hospital. But
I've got an Army jet bomber ready to fly West in about an
hour. You'll be on it. You'll go to Las Tiengas and work
alone."

"But the girl—"

"If she cracks, they may take her with them to Las Tiengas, too. As a decoy, a lure to bring her brother into the open. There's a better chance for you to find her and help her out there than if you stayed here and chased yourself in circles for Swayney. I'll call Mike Larabee, the security chief at Las Tiengas. You can check in with him. After that, you'll be on your own."

Durell stood up. "Thank you. I'm grateful."

"There isn't much time. I'll tell you something else. There's something wrong out there at the Las Tiengas Base. I can smell it. Something stinks in all this. Don't trust anybody. That's a hell of a thing to say, but that's the way I want you to play it. If you latch on to anything, don't contact anybody but me. No matter what it is." Blue eyes burned at Durell. "Do you understand?"

"Yes."

"Good luck, then," said McFee. "You'll need it. Officially, you're *persona non grata* for having lost contact with the girl. You know what happens if you miss." McFee sighed. "I'd hate to have to accept your resignation, Sam."

Durell nodded. "Is there time to see Sidonie Osbourn?" he asked.

McFee sighed. "God help her, yes."

The little house near Alexandria looked the same. He thought it ought to look different, somehow, but he could not see any change in it, and he knew that any difference he felt was in his mind, in the knowledge of permanent absence and loss. There was a neatly trimmed lawn, a low privet hedge, children playing a few houses away up the sloping curve of the street. It was cooler here than in Washington, which seemed to gather in a peculiar heat of its own. There were a few cars parked by the curb, none in front of the house. Durell got out and walked up the brick path to the door.

It opened as he reached for the bell and Sidonie stood there. No tears, but her eyes were unnaturally bright. He remembered her eyes as vivacious, Gallic, with their slightly upturned slant. He remembered the way she had kissed Lew on the occasions when he had come here with Lew for dinner.

He kissed her cheek.

Her underlip trembled. "Thank you, Sam."

He felt awkward, hating this. "Are you all right?"

"No. Of course not. How could I be?" Then she said, "I'm sorry, Sam. Don't mind me."

He followed her inside. Everything was the same. Well, what did you expect? Lew isn't here, he won't ever be here again, but he's left this, this house and this girl and the twins. He wanted to smash something.

"I sent the girls to a neighbor's," Sidonie said. "Sam, don't look like that."

Strength from her, given to him. He was astonished. "Sid—"

"I know how you loved him," she said quietly.

"I wish I'd been there."

"I knew it was going to happen, someday."

Staring at her, he said, "You knew?"

"We both knew. It was always a question not of *if,* but *when.* Every day was a holiday, Sam. Can you understand?"

"No," he said.

"You think he was wrong to marry me? I know you think so. You talked about it to Lew so often. But he wasn't wrong. It was wonderful."

"How can you—"

"He did his job," she said. She sat down and folded her hands in her lap and looked at her wedding ring. A small girl. Strong and brave. He felt ashamed of his own weakness. "He did his job and he knew the danger in it and so did I. We accepted it and lived with it."

"What will you do? I know it's too soon—"

"It's all been arranged. I'm going to work for General McFee. He just called me."

He looked at his watch. He had twenty minutes to get to the airport. He stood up.

"I have to go."

She nodded, arose, and kissed him. "Lew always said you needed a girl. I wish—"

"No," he said, almost violently.

"Sam, I'm sorry for you."

He was surprised. "For me? Don't be, Sid."

"Come back soon. I need to talk to you."

"Is there anything I can get for you, that you need?"

"No. Thank you, Sam."

"Anything I can do . . ."

"Finish the job," she said. "For Lew."

Chapter Nine . . .

The plane was riding high through the night, trying to overtake the purple sunset. The earth was hidden beneath cotton clouds. The interior of the bomber was austere, stripped, a pattern of punched-out Duralumin girders painted gray, yellow, black. He was in a bucket seat where he could see the seven-man crew up forward, hunched over a fantastic series of lighted banked instruments. One of them yawned. None was curious about him.

A blond young airman second class worked his way back toward Durell. "Are you all right, sir?" A Mississippi drawl.

"Fine."

"You like some coffee, sir?"

"Yes, please. Thanks. Could you tell me where we are now?"

"Vicksburg, I reckon."

He thought of the mighty river below. Several hundred miles to the south, in the Cajun bayou country, was his grandfather, aboard the old hulk of the *Three Belles*. His mind spun back to the past and he remembered Bayou Peche Rouge and the general store when he was fourteen, and 'Toinette Deslabes, whose papa ran the store. 'Toinette he remembered well, the way she ate oranges, small white teeth biting into the pulp. He remembered a night in the Pass-a-Joix, across the bayou, when he and 'Toinette had walked along the *chenière* together and then stopped walking and sank to earth under the moss-dripping live oaks. There were awkward fumblings, the making of love for the first time, frightened and ashamed when he failed. He remembered the smell of her, the pungency of oranges, the way she had writhed, frustrated by his boyish failure, how she had come at him furiously with a knife and he had knocked her down and taken the knife

48

away; and then because she was no longer the aggressor, he was able to take her as he willed. Later, his grandfather had asked him what had happened, and he knew the sounds they had made had carried across the still black water, across the masses of water hyacinth. . . .

His stomach tightened. He thought of Deirdre Padgett. He saw her in his mind with the bullet-headed giant, tortured and in pain, hurt badly. He forced himself to shy away from the images.

Later, at Yale, there was a girl from Litchfield, in her beaver coat, in her little roadster, driving back through the icy, barren hills to her home for dinner after the football game. She had turned into a barway, parking in the dark among the frozen, crystal weeds, and torn off her fur coat, torn away the veneer of Radcliffe, and it had been awkward in the tiny car, and strange to sit at dinner later in the old colonial house, with the milk glass and antique copper and the huge fireplace, and feel her hand groping for him under the table while her parents discussed the Yale eleven and its chances against Harvard. . . .

Deirdre, he thought, wanting to forget her, unable to forget her, helpless to aid her wherever she was at this moment. He told himself there was nothing he could have done back there that Swayney wouldn't do. He told himself that McFee was right, that the men who had taken her might as easily manage to bring her to Las Tiengas tomorrow. It didn't do any good. He thought of her red flowing hair, her wide gray eyes, the courage in her that fought against the ugly haunting fears. He thought of her bitter anger, because her brother had been abused and served with injustice. She had known, in his apartment, that she had been mistaken. He had seen it dawn in her, the knowledge that she herself was not important, or her brother; not any of them. But it had come too late, this putting aside of personal feelings. She might be dead now.

The bomber flew on through the night.

There were no clouds over Texas, and the stars were like polished bits of silver in the night sky. Up ahead, the navigator was talking to the engineer, laughing about something, reminding the engineer of a fiasco with some girl in a San Francisco bar. The radioman volunteered a comparison between the girl in the bar and a Japanese girl he had known in Yokosuka. Their laughter was strong, easy, free, mingling with the vibration of power from the jet engines. They knew what their job was and they were doing it, asking no questions of their passenger.

Hearing the soft voices, the different accents from Maine to Mississippi, from Brooklyn to Houston, he felt a change come over him. Hearing the steady beat of the powerful engines, feeling the lift of the wings that spanned the earth and the sky and carried him across the continent in a matter of hours, he felt better.

He closed his eyes and slept.

The airport at Las Tiengas was new, raw, and busy. A white-helmeted MP with eyes like steel marbles met him at the bomber, asked his name, and guided him to an Army scout car parked in the restricted military area of the field. Durell did not object, although this was not what he had expected. In a matter of moments, they were skimming down a new highway across the flat desert floor, away from the gaudy glow of lights that marked the town.

They passed a white-and-black barrier manned by more MP's, and under the desert moon Durell saw the white blocky shapes of barracks, skeletal rocket launchers, a huge hangar, a glare of blue light from a cavernous machine shop. The MP who drove was not communicative. He seemed bored. The desert wind was chilly.

Mike Larabee was waiting for him in an office of the Base Administration Building. Larabee was a squat bulldog of a man, his jaw dark with unshaven beard, eyes bloodshot, face tired. His glance was hostile. His handshake was hard and quick.

"Sit down, Durell. Relax. Like something to eat?"

"I didn't expect to work out of here," Durell said.

"You don't. You're supposed to be on your own. But I guess McFee figured you needed some briefing. I don't like it a bit, I tell you. A thing like this needs organization, a lot of men working together. What can you hope to do alone?"

"I hope to find Calvin Padgett."

"Nuts. You'll only get in my hair."

"I'll try not to," said Durell.

"Well, I just don't like prima donnas," Larabee growled. He slapped a palm over his mouth and wiped his hand across the lower half of his face, pulling and distorting his flesh with his fingertips. He sighed deeply. "Sorry. I haven't had much sleep. We'll get along, Durell."

"You know that Padgett is still somewhere in the area?"

Larabee nodded. His face looked more like a bulldog's than ever as he jutted his jaw angrily. "The son-of-a-bitch. The screwed-up bastard. I'd like to ream him with a forty-five."

"How did he get away from you?"

"We found that out just a few hours ago. Through a drainage culvert. Of all the goddamn things. Down a man-hole and crawling for two, three hundred yards, popping up like a gopher outside the wire and the radar. My own damned fault. I ought to be hanged."

Durell relaxed a little. "Any leads to where he might be hiding out?"

"Just one. He didn't go into town often, but he had a girl there. Or a woman friend, you might say. Cora Neville."

"Local girl?"

"Just the richest dame in ten states. You can't touch her, Durell. Don't try. We've got trouble enough without making her squawk. But she's staked out, too. Not a sign of Padgett. We searched her ranch and the whole damned motel. He wasn't there."

"What motel?" Durell asked.

"The Salamander. It's just north of town, and you never saw a place like it. Forty bucks a day, cigarettes a buck a pack, four bits for a Kleenex. Jaguars and Cadillacs and a lot of rich, spoiled, useless people taking the desert air, sobering up for the next round. She fits the place like a glove, that Cora Neville. Cal Padgett was right friendly with her."

Durell's face looked thin and sharp. "How did he get to know a woman like that?"

Larabee shrugged meaty shoulders. "Ah, who knows? She picked him up in one of the Cactus Street joints, probably just for kicks. These scientists are temperamental. They work along nice and quiet for a time, hypnotized by their own genius; then all of a sudden they're tired of the recreation we give 'em—bridge and billiards and chess. Cal didn't often go on a toot, but when he did, it was a beaut. We always had a man with him, of course, to see about drinking or talking too much. Policy said to let 'em relax, so we did. Only thing my boy couldn't do was get under the bed with them."

"I'll check into the Salamander tonight," Durell said.

Larabee shot him a hard, angry look. "He isn't there. I guarantee it. I went through the place as if I was looking for a two-headed louse. The Governor called me on it, I got calls from a Senator and two Congressmen in Washington. Seems I went too far and too fast with Miss Neville and she doesn't like her guests distressed. She says she doesn't know where Cal is and doesn't care. He was only a passing fancy. She was amused by his boyish earnestness, she said. But very annoyed with him now for causing her a little difficulty."

Seated, Durell felt the floor tremble and heard the vibration and shuddering of window glass. His eardrums felt odd. He looked up and saw Larabee watching, not grinning, but dimly amused.

"You're a tenderfoot, all right."

Durell still felt the sensation of concussion, deep in the pit of his stomach. "What was that?"

"My little babies never sleep. They're got to test their playthings. What you just felt, mister, was about a million bucks of the taxpayers' dough blown into the sky for fireworks."

"They fire at night, too?"

"With Dr. John, you never know. Come on, I guess you want to meet him."

They went downstairs to a jeep, drove along a street between barracks, turned left past a towering structure that made little sense to Durell, and drove about two miles into the chill desert before they came to a tall building with an observation tower like the control tower of an airport. An elevator took them up to the glassed-in room.

Dr. John Padgett was like a giant eagle, a big, bony man with hunched shoulders and a long-nosed face and loose limbs. He sat beside an assistant in a smock, watching numerous dials on a bank of recording instruments. There was a humming sound in the big room. On John Padgett's face there was a mark of intelligence and deep suffering. A rugged, roughly knobbed walking stick rested beside his chair, and when he stood up he leaned heavily on it as he shook hands with Durell.

"Yes, Mike told me you were coming." He had a deep, deliberate voice. "I regret it is my young brother who is causing all this trouble."

"Well, maybe you can help me," Durell said.

"I've done all I can. But if there is anything more—"

"I'd just like to know what kind of argument Calvin had with you about the work going on here," Durell said.

His shot went home. He saw the quick glance John Padgett exchanged with Larabee. Then the physicist shrugged, and his bony shoulders emphasized his resemblance to a hunched, bedraggled eagle.

"Calvin was distraught. He was impetuous. He felt that an error had been made in the calculations for our device and insisted on checking and rechecking. We did so. And there was no error."

"I take it you are certain of that," Durell said.

"It is my responsibility," John Padgett said quietly.

"I understand you considered Calvin as suffering from a nervous disorder of some kind. That right?"

"If you wish to speak to Dr. Crane about it—"

"You can tell me all I need to know," Durell said.

"Quite so. You know his history, of course—about the Investigating Committee and so forth. I could not bring myself to believe he harbored subversive notions. I took him under my personal parole, you might say. Perhaps it was a mistake. I dislike to think so, however, until every effort has been made to find Calvin. Our work here causes high mental strain among the staff, and a great deal of philosophical theorizing, you see. Calvin was growing steadily moodier, doubting the wisdom of our work. He was not alone in this, but others managed to keep their attitudes and fears under control. Calvin did not. He ran away. I am sure that when he is found, it will turn out to be no more than a gesture toward escape from reality."

John Padgett limped back to his instruments and studied them for a moment. Then he returned to Durell. His dark eyes burned with a fanatical light. "Whatever happens, nothing must interfere with the scheduled firing of Cyclops. It is my responsibility, above that of the military personnel here, above Mike Larabee's security forces, above everything except for certain people in Washington. I designed Cyclops, I helped to build it. It will succeed. It must succeed! I have put aside all personal feelings in regard to my brother. Whatever must be done about him I leave to your discretion. And now, if you will excuse me . . ."

Durell felt strangely disappointed. He did not know why he felt this way. Perhaps he was tired, he thought. This day had stretched out interminably. Then he looked up as Mike Larabee crossed the room, glanced at his watch, and tore a big sheet off a wall calendar.

It was past midnight. It was now the second day of July.

Chapter Ten . . .

He had no real difficulty getting a room at the Salamander.
Larabee had not exaggerated about the place. His room was
a cottage, discreetly apart from the others. He stopped in
Las Tiengas, which apparently knew no curfews, and rented
a car, then bought a suitcase and some clothing in the shops
on Cactus Street. Larabee did not come with him. Larabee
made it plain he did not like the idea of Durell's working
independently on the problem.

The town was built on flats slightly north of the center of
a forty-mile bowl rimmed by jagged buttes. Cactus Street
was noisy, lined with bars, lurid with neon, swarming with
military uniforms. Aloof from all this, like an oasis of plush
luxury, was the Salamander.

There was a main building surrounded by stately palms
and green lawns and oleanders. There was a huge swimming
pool, where some people still sat about in robes at tables
under umbrellas. There was a restaurant, a gambling room,
tennis courts, squash courts, a private auditorium for motion pictures, several shops, sun decks. The Salamander was
a world unto itself. Once here, the privileged guest need
not stir or want for anything. The cottages ranged in irregular patterns among more palm trees and shrubbery, discreetly located along private paths. The clerk's desk in the
lobby of the main building was like an upholstered doughnut, and the clerk went with the decor. His eyes at first
dismissed Durell briefly.

"Sorry, sir, we have absolutely nothing without a prior
reservation."

"I see," Durell said. "Then would you have a reservation
scheduled for tomorrow evening in the name of Miss Deirdre
Padgett?"

The clerk looked toward a winding, surrealistic staircase to a filigreed balcony above. A tall blonde woman was up there, talking to a dark-haired man in a dinner jacket. There were not many people in the lobby, but they all bore the same stamp: a deep tan, a haziness about the eyes from too much liquor and rich food, a poised and assured air of speaking and carriage. The clerk jerked his eyes back from the blonde woman above.

"Just a moment, sir. I'll see."

He slid out of the plush doughnut desk and walked up the airy staircase as if he wanted to run. He spoke to the blonde. She looked down at Durell. Her eyes were pale, either gray or blue, he could not tell which. Her oval face was darkly tanned, and her lipstick looked orange in the subdued lobby light. The handsome dark-haired man said something quickly and turned away. The blonde woman nodded to the desk clerk. Durell felt someone watching him and looked around and saw only a small, old Mexican in a red jacket and white trousers, a bellhop waiting for the new suitcase he had just purchased. He looked at the balcony again. The blonde, staggeringly beautiful, looked angry, like an annoyed goddess. The desk clerk all but tumbled down the filigreed staircase again.

"Yes, sir. I find we can accommodate you."

"Is that Miss Neville?"

"Why, yes, sir."

"You didn't answer my other question. About Miss Padgett."

"I'll check, sir."

"I thought you checked with Miss Neville."

The clerk was sweating, although the air in the lobby was pleasant and perfumed. "Just one moment."

When Durell looked up at the balcony, Cora Neville had vanished. The clerk consulted a file of extravagantly engraved cards, or pretended to consult them. Then he bobbed his head. "Yes, sir. A reservation exists for Miss Padgett, of Washington, D.C., for tomorrow. Is she a friend of yours, sir?"

"Yes, indeed."

"Your cottage is number Twenty-three. I hope you will be comfortable."

Service at the Salamander was supplied by Mexicans, and the elderly bellhop, whose name was Miguel, took Durell's suitcase while a smart young man parked Durell's rented car and a liquid-eyed girl smiled and turned down the coverlet on his bed. He ordered ice and a bottle of bonded bourbon and a sandwich, and when all this had been quietly and quickly delivered, he took a hot shower and ate the sandwich and had a quick drink.

Yet he felt he was not alone.

He turned out the lights and adjusted the slats of the blinds and sat still in the darkness, smoking, finishing his second drink. His nerves felt stretched to the breaking point. Ahead, through the hours, there seemed to be nothing to do but wait.

He got up and went outside and stood in the cool desert air, in the deep shadow of the oleander bush beside the cottage door. There was nothing to see. The nearest cottage, of which only a corner was visible down the curving path, was in darkness. He walked around the small stuccoed building, looking at the dark shrubbery. Nobody was there.

But he was watched.

The bourbon had not helped. His nerves still hummed. He stretched out on the bed in the dark and tried to sleep. He could not sleep. Somewhere nearby was Calvin Padgett, alone as he was alone, maybe frightened, certainly confused. In his head, a knowledge of the stars in their courses, and a change in the heavens to be made within about forty hours. Not much time. Durell tossed and turned. He was here, but Deirdre was not here, and nothing could flush Padgett from his hiding place until the girl arrived. *If* she arrived. If she wasn't dead by now. He hoped she had sense enough to talk just enough to make them bring her out here. There was nothing he could do about it, though, except to wait. And hope.

Something occurred to him. He could take Larabee's word for it that Calvin Padgett was not hidden at the Salamander. Then how did Padgett expect to know when his sister arrived? She was due tomorrow—no, this evening. How would Padgett know about it? Durell sat up, his nerves suddenly tight. Somebody would have to tell Padgett, wherever he was hiding, that his sister had arrived. Assuming Deirdre had told him all of the truth, and there was nothing more prearranged between sister and brother. But you had to assume that. And if so, then someone here knew where Padgett was hiding. Someone here was watching the register, waiting for

Deirdre to check in. Not just Larabee's men, either. One of the staff? Or Cora Neville? He felt impatient for daylight, for the day to begin, so that he could check. He wanted to meet Cora Neville. He wanted to look over the staff. All right. Somebody here knew where Calvin Padgett, the most wanted man in history, was hiding.

And somebody was watching him.

The feeling was so strong that again Durell got up and took his gun and stepped outside to circle the cottage. Nobody. Nothing. A dry breeze made the palm fronds rustle and clack. He went inside and turned on the lights and opened the closet doors and looked in the shower stall. No one. He went back to bed.

To wait for Deirdre's arrival, if she ever got here, meant an intolerable delay. Time was too precious, running out too fast. He could not just sit here and wait. He had to force something to happen. He knew that his inquiry about Deirdre had started something back there in the lobby. He wondered about the man who had been with Cora Neville. This was a lever that Larabee, with all his security organization, had not possessed on his previous check of this place. Larabee had not known about Deirdre Padgett. The fact that there actually was a reservation for Deirdre gave Durell a sudden new hope. He knew he would not have to wait for her arrival. Something was going to happen sooner than that.

And then suddenly he was asleep.

When he awoke, he sensed at once that someone else was in the room.

He did not move. He held his breath.

The dim stirring sound came to him. He had an awareness of an hour, perhaps two, having passed. He was surprised at the suddenness with which he had slept. He tasted the bourbon in his mouth. He listened.

The cottage consisted of the bedroom, the living area, and a peach-tiled bath. Darkness prevailed when he opened his eyes. Someone moved softly in the living area beyond the door. He heard a faint click. It was the catch on his suitcase. Still he did not move.

· Now he heard breathing, short and quick, anxious and a little fearful. He slid his hand under the pillow and closed his fingers around his gun. He felt better. He liked this. He was eager to see who the intruder might be. But he took his time about moving.

The sounds of the search went on, muted, woven through the dry clacking of the palm fronds in the desert wind outside. Everything else was still. Durell slid from the bed to his feet and reached the door. And the sounds stopped.

"Hold it," Durell said. "Just as you are."

He snapped on the light switch. It was almost a fatal mistake. In the prompt brilliant glare, he was blinded. There was a blur of movement as someone darted toward the cottage door. He almost fired. Sharply he said, *"Alto!"*

It was the old Mexican, Miguel, who had carried his bags.

His suitcase stood open on the couch, the new shirts he had bought tumbled about. The old man stood still and trembled. He had a thick gray mustache, thick gray hair. The trim little red jacket he wore looked undignified for his years.

"Señor, por favor—"

Durell spoke quietly in Spanish, to put him at ease. "Come back here. Sit down. You will not be harmed."

"It was a mistake, señor. I beg of you, it was a mistake."

"We will see. Sit down."

The old man's eyes touched Durell's gun, scurried over Durell's face, and he sat down stiffly, uncomfortably, embarrassed to be seated in the cottage on the fine furniture. Durell lit a cigarette, poured some bourbon, and drank it, letting the silence build upon itself while the old man's nervousness grew. Great beads of sweat stood out on Miguel's flat brow, on the fine, sunburned planes of his old face.

"Tell me about your mistake," Durell said.

"I forgot myself. I am an old man. I thought this cottage was not occupied. I was looking for—something."

Durell smiled. "Go on."

"I cannot go on."

"You are a poor liar, Miguel."

"Yes."

"You should not have been entrusted with this mission."

"I did not desire it, señor. I am not a thief."

"Who sent you to search my things?"

"There has been much searching and looking, much police activity in the past two days. It is nothing new."

"But you are not the police," Durell said. "Who sent you?"

The old man shivered. He closed his eyes. He sat with his hands on his knees, his shoulders bowed. Yet there was a dignity in him that came through the red monkey jacket, the slick white trousers, the polished black shoes. The dignity was in his work-worn hands, the lined face, the dark eyes that had seen so much.

"You must tell me," said Durell, "or I shall go to the management with my complaint. To Miss Neville."

"No, please! Not to her!"

"Why not?"

"I will be discharged," Miguel said slowly. "Are you also from the police? When I carried your suitcase, it was too light for a traveler. And your clothing is not the sort of clothing one wears in the desert. You have come from far away, suddenly, without preparation."

"You are an astute man," Durell said, nodding.

"But I wanted to be certain. I did not trust my thinking. I had to see for myself, with my own eyes. You are of the police, señor?"

"No," Durell said. "Not of those you have seen here before. Why should you be interested in me, whatever my clothing or luggage?" When the old man did not answer, Durell stood up, pretending impatience. "Come along. We will go to see Miss Neville."

"At this hour? It is three o'clock. She will be very angry."

"I, too, am angry," Durell said. "You are stupid. If you would trust me, we might each accomplish our mission successfully. Since you do not, we shall see what Miss Neville has to say."

The old man seemed about to speak, then was silent. He stood up as if he was tired in every bone of his old body. Durell was disappointed. He had suddenly been sure that Miguel was the contact Padgett had hoped to use to reach his sister when she arrived. *If* she arrived. But it was too much to hope for. Maybe the old man was merely a petty thief. He certainly was not working with Cora Neville, or acting under her direction. His reluctance to be taken to face her was genuine.

Durell slid his feet into his shoes and let the old Mexican precede him from the cottage. Overhead, the desert stars glittered and gleamed. The stars in their courses, unchanging, eternal, he thought. Not any more. His shoes grated on the fine gravel of the winding path that led past other dark cottages. There were lights still on in the central building of the Salamander layout, but only from the tall glass doors of the stone lobby entrance and one other window, which was partly shaded, on the third floor in the rear. The wind felt cold.

Durell halted. "Does Miss Neville live here all the time, Miguel?"

"She has a ranch in the Tiengas Hills. It is about twenty miles from here." The old Mexican's voice was suddenly harsh. "But that is her apartment, up there with the lighted window at the balcony you see. She is there now. With Señor West, no doubt."

"West?"

"He is the manager of the Salamander, but he is more than that to Miss Neville. Perhaps I should not say it, señor. It is not my business."

Durell said abruptly, "I understood she was in love with a young man named Calvin Padgett."

The name seemed to hang on the edge of the desert wind. There was a silence. Durell waited.

Miguel said, "Yes. He has been here several times."

"Then you know him?"

"He is a good young man."

"Do you know of his sister?"

Miguel's eyes were liquid white in the dark shadow of the shrubbery where they had halted. His breath made a soft hissing sound. "Señor, do not ask anything of me. I am a simple man. I do not understand all this. I have a feeling you may be a friend, but I cannot trust my feelings in this matter. I must do what I am told."

"Then you know where Calvin Padgett is?"

"The police also asked me that. I told them nothing. To them I am an ignorant old Mexican."

"But I am asking you. For Padgett's sister."

"I can tell you nothing."

"Would you consider Miss Neville a friend of Padgett's?"

The answer was sharp and vehement. "No, señor. Never. Whatever the young man hopes, she is not for him. She is a snake, she is a sorceress. She is all evil. But he cannot be advised in this, for he will not believe such things about her."

Durell drew a deep breath. He looked up at the lighted window. There was no one else in sight at this hour, anywhere on the lavishly landscaped grounds of the Salamander.

The wind whimpered in the shrubbery, rattled the palm fronds, blew sand from the crouching desert.

"Will you tell Calvin Padgett of me?" Durell asked.

"I cannot, señor. I do not know where he is."

"But you are his friend."

"I talk too much, and it is the babbling of an old man. I am sorry if I misled you, señor. I cannot help you find him."

Durell looked sharply at the old Mexican. He thought Miguel was lying, but he could not be sure. He had come fast and hard, this far; now suddenly the old man was blocking him. He had accomplished much more than Larabee in his two days of search; but he'd had the advantage of knowing about the contact set up with Deirdre.

"Why did you search my room, Miguel? I ask you again."

"I was curious about you because at the desk when you registered you inquired about a reservation for the Señorita Padgett. I was curious, but it was a mistake."

Durell nodded. He had guessed right about the reason for his progress. "Miss Neville did not send you?"

"No, señor, I swear it."

Somewhere, Durell thought, he had slipped. He had almost won the old man's confidence, but now Miguel had retreated, guarding his answers, standing hunched in the cold night wind. Maybe Miguel was on the other side of the fence. He told himself to take nothing for granted.

"All right, Miguel. You can go now."

"Señor, I am in your debt for not reporting me."

"Go along."

The old Mexican bobbed his head and shuffled away out of sight. Durell watched him go. He looked up at the bright stars again and was annoyed because he shivered. Then, when he was sure he was alone, he turned toward the main building of the Salamander. It was time to push another button to make things happen.

Chapter Eleven . . .

He moved like a shadow, like a stalking panther, like a falling leaf. In ten minutes, by means of an outside stairway, a dimly lighted, scented corridor, and another stairway, he stood in the darkness of the balcony that was not quite darkness, slitted by the light through the Venetian blinds of Cora Neville's window. Voices moved out to him on the whimpering desert wind. The intensity of their anger touched him through the woman's voice and he stood like a shadow among the other balcony shadows, looking into the apartment within.

He saw a bedroom, elegantly feminine, pink and gold and ivory and ebony. A huge swan bed, Florentine mirrors, gilt Renaissance tables, delicate chairs. Mirrors that flashed and winked and reflected the scene a score of times over, at intricate angles and perspectives.

Cora Neville sat at a vanity table, studying her blonde erotic beauty. From the waist up she was nude, and around her swelling hips was a slithered heap of silk, nothing more. Her nakedness did not seem to be a conscious matter with her, or designed to gain any overt reaction from the man who was with her. The man was the general manager of the Salamander, George West, tall and lithe, with a dark face and darker rage, who moved in the room with an intimacy that made their relationship clear at once, the intimacy of husband and wife, or lovers long grown domestic with each other.

Durell watched and wondered.

They were not speaking in English. They were using German. Durell had learned German well when he had been with Lew Osbourn in Cologne.

". . . nothing to be done. Better to know where he is, so he can be watched."

"It is an unnecessary risk!"

"George, you are losing your nerve." The woman's face was lovely and cold and full of hate.

The man walked across the room and put his hands on the woman's shoulders, looking at her reflected in all the mirrors. His hands were casual, intimate, stroking her body. The woman looked at him with nothing at all in her gray eyes. But her shoulders shrank a little, and the man felt her shrinking under his hands, and he smiled.

"Perhaps you are right. Perhaps he comes from the sister, after all."

"Please, George."

He said something in another language, not German. Durell thought it was Czech. He did not understand it. He stood blended with the shadows in the wind on the balcony, frustrated. They had been talking about him and about the woman's decision to let him have a cottage here. The man was dubious. Durell looked more closely at the man, his wide forehead, thin nose, slitted mouth, dark hair. In his early forties, built like a bull, hard and tanned, with black glowing eyes. He had moved away from the half-naked woman. His anger deepened his scowl. Now suddenly they spoke in English.

"Cora, we must not make a mistake about this. If I am successful, you will be rid of me for good and always."

"That will be nice," the woman said dryly.

"You will not betray me, darling, or your life as you know it will be at an end. Must I repeat what will happen to you if our liaison of the past years becomes known to the authorities?"

"You've said it often enough. I know that you are low enough to destroy me."

"Strong enough. Put it that way. We must find Calvin Padgett. Surely he will contact you soon. When the sister arrives, you must be alert."

"And the man? This Durell? What of him?"

"I'll take care of him," said West.

"Will you kill him?"

"It may not be necessary," West said, shrugging.

"When does the girl arrive?"

"Tomorrow."

Silent in the shadows of the balcony, Durell heard them switch again to Czech or Hungarian, whatever it was. The man turned out several of the lights in the room, then approached the seated woman. His hands moved over her. She sat quietly and submissively, permitting his attentions. Sand slithered over the stone balcony floor, hissing, pushed by the wind.

Durell decided he had heard all that it was necessary to hear. Neither Cora Neville nor her threatening manager, George West, knew where to find Padgett. But they wanted very much to find him. And they knew about Deirdre's impending arrival, and its significance. That, too. He permitted himself a quick feeling of triumph at having come so far so soon. Larabee was not to be blamed for having seen no importance in the Salamander except that Calvin had been noted several times with its ornate owner. Yet Durell's luck made him feel apprehensive, as if it had come too quickly and easily. He still did not know where to find Padgett. And the hours stretched long and gray until Deirdre arrived. He was tempted for a moment to put everything in Larabee's hands. But that would be premature. He really had nothing, as yet. He did not have Calvin Padgett.

Shadow-silent, Durell drifted away from the window, down the balcony, down the steps, and back to his waiting cottage. Miguel was gone. He locked the door, checked out the windows, and sat on the bed in the darkness.

Now he began to shake.

He thought of Deirdre and the giant with the shaved head. He prayed she would talk quickly, before they hurt her too much.

His trembling grew worse.

If she talked, if she broke quickly, she would arrive here escorted by the bullet head. If not—

He found the bottle of bourbon and took another drink. It did nothing for him. He still shook. He told himself that he must not let Deirdre Padgett mean this much to him. He told himself that she was only a small part of the pattern unfolding inexorably before him. The wind whimpered around the cottage, blew through the palms, rustled in the shrubbery. It was already past four o'clock in the morning. He had not had any real sleep except for brief, troubled snatches back in Washington before Lew was killed, and on the plane that brought him here. But he was not tired, nor was he sleepy. He reached for a cigarette.

Another drink was a temptation, but he put it from him.

He took a hot shower instead, and then he shaved. The windows were gray with dawn. He watched the daylight come, and he waited.

From the aquamarine tiled pool, he could watch the ornate entrance to the Salamander grounds and the crushed stone driveway that swept up to the lobby door. The desert sun was incredible, a burning weight on his bare chest and shoulders. Durell had bought a pair of swim trunks, adding thirty dollars to his bill, wondering if he would have to pay this himself. Although it was eleven o'clock in the morning, not too many of the guests had appeared yet. Several women in bathing suits that would not have been allowed on public beaches lay on air mattresses, their fine legs and pampered bodies oiled and glistening, little jeweled nose guards and dark glasses protecting what they wanted to protect. They looked at Durell with interest and invitation, but he ignored them. Now and then he watched the Mexican help move quickly and silently to answer a summons for breakfast or a hangover cure from one of the cottages. Quite a few of the breakfasts were solely liquid.

Over everything was the bright sun, the heat, the dry clear air. Twice Durell felt concussions that meant a rocket was being tested twenty or thirty miles away to the south, in the restricted government testing area. Nobody paid any attention.

There were no new arrivals.

Occasionally a station wagon came and went, or a little MG, and once a Rolls departed, carrying the regal personage of an aging Hollywood actress. He wondered how they planned to bring Deirdre here, once she talked; *if* she talked. Probably by private plane, landing somewhere in the desert. No difficulty there. Durell lay on his stomach and sweated. And she did not come.

He saw Miguel carrying a breakfast tray, his thick gray hair shining in the brilliant sunshine. Migual looked through him and hurried on.

He watched the chambermaids, slim light-footed girls with beautiful carriage and dark olive skins, moving silently from cottage to cottage, doing their work. There were more people at the pool now. A group sat near him, talking too loudly, their accents British and Newport and too shrill. The women looked anxious and tense and unhappy. The men were bored.

Lying there in the brutal glare of the sun, he felt again that someone was watching him.

He lifted his head and turned, feeling the sweat on his skin pull at the air mattress under him. He saw long, firm, tanned legs, a short striped jacket that gave the illusion that there was no clothing under it. Cora Neville stood with her eyes hidden behind green harlequin glasses, a cigarette in one hand.

"Mr. Durell?"

He started to rise, and she waved him down and sank to the mattress beside him. There came a shriek of laughter from the pool and she looked that way, smiling, before turning to him again. Her movements were graceful, studied, and mechanical. Her blonde hair looked almost white against the dark tan of her face.

"You must forgive me," she said, "for intruding on your solitude. I am Cora Neville. The Salamander is mine. I hope you are comfortable?"

"I'd be a dog if I said I wasn't," Durell replied.

She smiled. It was a stretching and twitching of tiny muscles at the corners of her perfect mouth, nothing more.

"You slept well, then," she said.

"Of course."

"While you are here, you must make use of our facilities. We have saddle horses, games of all kinds, the finest restaurant between New Orleans and San Francisco. If you are lonely, we can even arrange to take care of that." The smile again, meaning nothing. "Do you plan to stay with us long?"

"Perhaps until the Fourth of July," Durell said.

Nothing happened.

There was more shrieking from the big kidney-shaped pool.

Cora Neville smoked, dragging deeply at the cigarette. It was all that betrayed her. She said, "Mr. Durell, I trust you are not from the police."

He pretended surprise. "That's an odd remark to make to a guest."

"I am a busy woman, Mr. Durell. I must be sure. I have made my position plain enough. Will you be equally frank with me?"

"I'm not from the police," Durell said.

"But you are working with them, or for them, in the matter of Cal Padgett. You inquired about Calvin's sister last night when you registered. I should have refused you accommodations then, but I am tired of arguing with Colonel Larabee about it. I have influential friends. I told Larabee so. I can use that influence to have you thrown out of here on a moment's notice, Mr. Durell."

He watched the entrance, not meaning to have his attention distracted if Deirdre arrived. The gateway was empty. Under other circumstances, he would have been enjoying himself. Cora Neville was easily the most beautiful woman he had seen for a long time. Her hip-length jacket was open now, and he saw she was wearing a burgundy bathing suit, remarkably modest in view of what seemed to be the vogue around him. He looked at the gate again.

"She isn't here yet," Cora said bluntly.

"But you expect her?"

"We have her reservation in our files, as you know. Are you well acquainted with Miss Padgett?"

"I've never met her."

She said, too casually, "But you know what she looks like?"

"Tall redhead, beautiful."

"Yes." She seemed relieved. "Calvin spoke of her often. I wish to impress upon you, Mr. Durell, that I will not tolerate a scene here. I cannot afford to divert my guests that way. As for my relations with Calvin, I have already explained them many times to Colonel Larabee. It was nothing. He was a young man I took a temporary liking to, nothing more."

"Was?" Durell asked.

She looked puzzled, then shrugged. "I think of him in the past, because nothing came of it. He thought he was in love with me, but it was a mistake. We had fun for a few weeks, the few times he called for me. Nothing more than that. I know you people are looking for him, but I can't help you. I don't know what he's done or why he seems to be so terribly important to you. I don't know where he is now."

"I believe you," Durell said.

Now she was surprised. She tried to hide it by playing with the cigarette. Durell took it from her fingers and crushed it out in an ash tray at the edge of the pool. A girl swam by, splashed water at him, laughed, and dived away. It was getting quite noisy at the Salamander now as more guests revived. Miguel went by. His eyes looked reptilian for the moment they rested on Cora Neville. The woman did not notice him, any more than she noticed the palm trees, the shrubbery, the discreet cottages, the people in the pool.

"I wish—" she began.

Durell waited.

Her mouth shook.

He glanced in the direction she was looking, and he saw the manager, George West, standing on the wide shallow steps of the lobby entrance, his tanned face alert, hard, dangerous.

"You were going to say something," Durell reminded her.

Cora Neville stood up. "It was nothing."

"What are you afraid of?" he asked.

She looked down at him. "It's so easy to feel safe, when you have everything behind you, when all the money and power and energy have molded you and made you conform. But if you stumble, if you fall out of line, what then, Mr. Durell? Then you are afraid, isn't it so?"

"Are you out of line?" he asked.

"I'm out of my mind," she said, and walked away from him, toward the man who stood on the steps, watching.

The kind of work you do, Durell thought, is like that of an infantryman during a war. There are moments of intense activity, the heart-hammering excitement of an instant's action, and then there is the waiting. You've waited before, waited and watched, and let the hours go by in patience, in the sure knowledge of your business, which is mostly this waiting and watching.

But this waiting is different. Why? You stretch out here in the incredible sun by this pool under a desert sky and idle people around you accept you and step over you and talk about you or ignore you. But your heart lurches, your stomach is knotted, you stretch your fingers and watch them tremble. And you wonder why.

You saw her only briefly, for only a few minutes. At first she hated you and then she tolerated you and at last she trusted you. What makes her different from all the other women you have known? You might as well ask why oxygen and hydrogen make water instead of oil. There is no reason for this. It just exists. It came into being when you first saw her, standing like a doe at bay on that street in Washington. How long ago? Only a day. Or a lifetime. But it is there. When you think that they may have hurt her, or killed her, then you feel a lust to avenge, and this is not the way you have been trained, which was to analyze with a cool mind and a detached heart, so you may judge your moves correctly and live.

Suddenly Durell was sure she was dead, that they had killed her. They would have tortured her, but she would not have spoken. She was not coming. He stood up, and suddenly Miguel was there before him, a drink in his hand. The old Mexican's face was bland, unsmiling.

"Your bourbon, señor."

"I ordered nothing."

"Please take the drink. They are watching. I must have some excuse to talk to you, do you understand?"

"What?" Durell said. Sickness surged in him. And hate. And anger. "What are you saying?"

"She is here, señor. The Señorita Padgett."

Durell looked at the gateway. A dusty, sand-stained station wagon was parked by the lobby steps. A man got out of it and Durell's heart began to hammer. It was the giant with the bullet head. The man who had killed Lew Osbourn.

Then the girl stepped out, her head high, calm and poised. Red hair caught the highlights of the desert sun and glowed with copper. Long legs moved easily up the steps beside the crop-headed giant.

She looked enough like Deirdre Padgett to have been her sister, perhaps, or a camera stand-in.

But she was not Deirdre.

They had rung in a double.

They had killed her.

Chapter Twelve . . .

Now he was cold and deadly calm. Now he knew what had to be done. Nothing was going to stop him. He left the pool and went back to his cottage and dressed with care, checked his gun and cartridges, and rang for service. The telephone in the cottage was a temptation to call Larabee, to dump it in Larabee's lap. But he wanted no one to share this with him. It was something he had to do alone. For Lew and for the girl. The ringer did not interest him. She was merely a decoy, and probably innocent of the meaning of what her role called for. She was only the lure that would make Calvin Padgett expose himself. She could be ignored.

Miguel came in answer to his summons. The little Mexican slipped into the cottage quietly, bobbed his head, and waited.

He spoke in Spanish. "Sit down, Miguel."

"It is not permitted. You wish to order something?"

"I said to sit down."

The old man sat on the edge of the couch. Alarm touched his dark, aged eyes. "Is something wrong?"

"Very wrong. Have you notified Calvin Padgett that his sister has arrived?"

"I do not know what you are talking about."

Durell said earnestly, "Miguel, listen to me. There is not much time. A trick has been played upon you and me and upon our mutual friend, the young man I seek."

"A trick?"

"The young woman who arrived here twenty minutes ago, escorted by a murderer, is not Deirdre Padgett."

Miguel lurched to his feet. His face twisted. "You are lying to me, señor."

"I am not lying. Do I look as if I am lying?"

"But if what you say is so—"

71

"The true sister must be dead," Durell finished for him.

Miguel's face was gray. "They would not do such a thing."

"They would. They have. They have killed my best friend. They have killed the girl. The one who arrived here is an actress, paid to impersonate Deirdre Padgett, so that Calvin will reveal himself. Do you understand now?" Durell heard the sound of his voice, harsh and brazen in the cottage. He spoke more softly. "Have you called Calvin and said that his sister has arrived?"

"Yes, señor," Miguel whispered.

"Then you must take me to him."

"But—"

"At once."

"I promised—"

Durell took out his gun. He pointed it at the old man. "Do you wish to die, Miguel?"

"I am not afraid of death. I am at peace with God."

"Get up," Durell said. "Take me to Padgett."

Miguel arose wearily. His eyes touched the gun, then Durell's face. "You were in love with the sister, señor?"

"I don't know. Yes. Why do you ask?"

"It is in your eyes. I am sorry, señor."

"Let's go," Durell said.

Miguel nodded. "Yes. I will take you. But they will see us leave. There is no other driveway out of the Salamander, except by the main gate. And they will be watching. They will follow us."

"We'll lose them. Come."

Durell's rented car was parked in the shade beside the cottage. The sunlight was blinding. Miguel got in as Durell started the motor. Heat struck at him as he drove down the winding driveway to the entrance. He did not drive too fast. People strolled in the way, wearing tennis shorts, bathing suits, all sorts of sports garb. Everyone was leisurely. He saw everything as if the world moved like a slow-motion film.

From the gate, Miguel directed him south onto the main highway that led to Las Tiengas. Neither spoke. There was heavier traffic as they neared the town, and they passed two military convoys. Now and then Durell looked back in the mirror to see if they were being followed. There was nothing suspicious in sight.

Las Tiengas baked in the blazing sun. On Cactus Street the bars were open and thriving, the slot machines whirred, the crowds on the sidewalk milled and surged back and forth. Most of the populace consisted of construction workers and military personnel and their families. There was almost a wartime air of frenetic excitement about the place, although two years ago the town had been nothing but a whistle stop on a little-used branch of the Southern Pacific.

"We are being followed," Miguel said.

"Which car?"

"The green foreign car. Señor West is driving. Two others are with him."

Durell saw the rakish green sedan in the rear-view mirror. "What is our destination?"

"My home," Miguel said. "Calvin is there."

"Do they have your address at the Salamander?"

"It is possible, yes. Can we lose them, señor?"

"We'll try," Durell said. "You direct me."

"My house is in the Mexican quarter, to the south of the city. You turn at the next traffic light, go for four streets, then turn right. My house is the third one."

"You live alone?"

"Yes, señor."

Durell did not turn at the traffic light. He went on, checking the green car behind him. It did not turn, either. He felt more hopeful. He waited for the next traffic light, then turned north, tramped on the gas, and roared down a street busy with bars and shops. He turned at the next corner, shot into an alley, twisted out and doubled back. The green car was still behind him. He could see West's face over the driver's wheel, dark glasses glinting in the sun. They were much nearer now.

Durell swung south. He jumped a light, heard a blare of outraged auto horns, rocketed down a side street, twisted south again, turned once more, and drove the car into an alley. Sirens wailed far behind him.

"Out, Miguel."

The old Mexican moved fast. They were at the corner, in deep shade, under an awning outside a *frutería* in the Mexican quarter. The green car went by fast, looking for them. Durell saw the three men in it very clearly, but they did not see him. They went on past the alley and did not come back.

"This way, señor."

Miguel trotted down the sidewalk. There were small, poor

houses on this street, dominated by a fine old Spanish mission church. There was a small square that could have been anywhere in Mexico, and then a narrow side street, and Miguel stopped at the third house from the corner.

The front door stood open.

Dark, empty shadows yawned inside.

Miguel said something in rapid Spanish that Durell did not catch, and started forward. Durell held him back with a hand on his arm.

"How many rooms?"

"Two only."

"I will go first."

He moved in fast, but he knew there would be no danger now. The open door told him all that was needed. The rooms were small, immaculately clean, with white-washed walls and heavy, ornate furniture. They were empty. No one was here.

Calvin Padgett was gone.

The bed in the back room was unmade, and there was a litter of cigarette butts in a souvenir ash tray of Los Angeles. One entire wall of the bedroom served as a kitchen and cooking area. There was a heavy wooden table across from the bed, near the kerosene stove, and papers were scattered and torn upon the walnut surface. Durell picked them up, hearing Miguel's tight, tired breathing. The sheets of paper were covered with all sorts of mathematical symbols, formulae, and computations that were meaningless to Durell. Great heavy lines had been drawn across the equations, as if they had proved useless. Durell gathered them up and put them all in his pocket.

Miguel looked tortured. "It is my fault. I acted hastily. I heard them speak of the girl's arrival, and then I saw her and telephoned to the *frutería* to have them tell Calvin that his sister had arrived at last. How was I to know she was not the true one he waited for? Señor, are you sure—"

"It's not your fault, Miguel."

He tried to think. He dismissed the idea that Padgett had stepped out of the house only temporarily. Padgett had been waiting impatiently for word from Miguel about Deirdre, and he had acted promptly. What had he done, where had he gone? Not to the Salamander, or Durell would not have been followed as tenaciously as he had been. Where, then? Think. Don't make any mistakes. Padgett would have called the Salamander to speak to Deirdre. The switchboard girl would have been readied for the call, quick to notify Cora Neville. What then? Would Padgett have insisted on speaking to his sister, personally? Likely. Better than that. Almost certain. And? They would have had to put the ringer on the other end of the line. Would they? No choice, if Padgett insisted hard enough. And Padgett was not taking any chances. Whatever his game, whatever these calculations meant, whatever his reason for causing this man-hunt, he was playing it smart and careful. Small wonder Larabee could not find him, hidden away here in the Mexican quarter.

Durell walked to the open front door. The street was empty, blazing with sunlight. A woman in a black dress walked to the corner grocery. So Padgett had called, demanded to speak to his sister. They'd had to put the ringer on the phone, prompting her with what to say. But Padgett wouldn't have been fooled by that. He'd have known at once that it wasn't Deirdre. He'd give the Salamander a wide berth after that. He'd know that the others were after him, that a trap was set for him at the Salamander. So he wouldn't go there. Nor would he dare to stay here in this neighborhood, where his call might be traced.

Padgett would fly to sanctuary. Who would he trust? To whom would he turn at this crisis?

Cora Neville.

But he'd stay clear of the Salamander.

"Miguel."

"Yes, señor?"

"You said Miss Neville has a ranch somewhere?"

"Yes. In the Tiengas Hills. Twenty miles from here. You go north out of town, and when you come to a dirt road with a sign, you turn right. It is a horse ranch, but she does not live there very much." Miguel's face was gray. "You think Calvin went there?"

"No other place." Durell spoke quickly. "You must help me. We will need others. Use the telephone at the *frutería,* and call the Army base and ask for Colonel Larabee. You will speak for me, do you understand?"

Miguel nodded. "And what shall I say?"

"You will tell Larabee everything that has happened. Do not be afraid of punishment for helping Padgett. You will tell Larabee I have gone to Cora Neville's ranch and that he is to come and help me at once."

"You go alone?"

Durell nodded. "You will also tell Larabee that he is to pick up the manager of the Salamander, the man who calls himself George West. Tell the Colonel that George West is really a wanted agent named Gustav Weederman." Durell drew a deep breath. He could be wrong, but he didn't think so. The man with the bullet head had thought Padgett had double-crossed Weederman, and had mentioned the name to Deirdre back in Washington. Swayney thought Weederman was dead. Durell did not believe it. Neither did he believe that Padgett had really made a deal with Weederman. Everything that had happened pointed the other way, to a mix-up among the enemy as to where Padgett stood. Maybe Cora Neville had been too sure of herself in reporting to the others, or had colored her story in her favor.

"Go now," he said to Miguel.

He waited until the old Mexican trotted across the square toward the fruit store. Then he walked quickly in the other direction, to the alley where he had left his car.

Driving north from Las Tiengas, he saw how it all fitted together. Somewhere in the past, Cora Neville had been indiscreet; perhaps in Europe. Perhaps a love affair with Weederman. She had made it plain in the conversation Durell had overheard last night that she was an unwilling accomplice. Weederman, as George West, had forced her to give him the position as manager at the Salamander. A fine spot for an espionage agent, where high-ranking officers from the base came to relax, maybe to drink and talk too much about their hardware. It figured. It fitted. Cora Neville had played for Padgett deliberately, on orders from West. Padgett still did not know the truth. Cora, anxious to please, anxious to get out from whatever hold Weederman had over her, did as she was told. All right. The thing now was to get Padgett out of the box they had fitted for him. He did not let himself think too much about Deirdre.

The road was an empty ribbon unwinding under him. It was two o'clock when he spotted the sign, in the shape of a horse, and the arrow to the right. The country was barren and desolate, with stratified hills rising at sharp angles from the desert valley. It was a country of lizards and rattlesnakes and death.

He drove more slowly now, between rusted barbed-wire fences, climbing steadily. A few trees struggled to live in the narrow canyons opening on either hand, and then abruptly the countryside was greener, with grass on the slopes and a grove of cottonwoods here and there at the site of brief mountain springs. Another sign indicated a left turn onto what was obviously a private road. Durell drove on beyond it, found an outcropping of red rock, hid the car there, and walked back.

Five minutes of walking brought him in sight of the ranch house, a low spreading structure of dun-colored stone and glass, built into the hill. Horses moved in a pasture beyond. He saw a corral, a barn that was also built of stone, and several outbuildings. The green foreign car was parked in front of the main house.

Durell halted to study the terrain. In the silence he heard the sudden neighing of a palomino, the piping of a bird, the gurgle of water, the hum of a Diesel power generator. The sky was a brassy bowl of heat pressing down between the distorted hills. No one was in sight. Nobody had followed him.

He saw a trail that led up behind a butte, and he climbed it, hugging the rocks and shadows. Heat reflected from the stone and shale and made the sweat roll off him. He took the gun from its holster and held it in his hand. Once he had to climb a paddock fence, and another time a dog came barking at him, but with tail wagging, and he let the dog sniff at his trousers. Satisfied, the animal trotted away.

Ten minutes passed before he crawled flat on his stomach to the overhang of rock beyond the stone barn. From here he could see the road winding down the valley toward the desert. There was no sign of Larabee.

Voices drifted up to him, but he could not locate their source. Then a door slammed and he saw Cora Neville walking from the barn toward the house. She was almost running. Her blonde hair was burnished by the blazing sun. Then a man came after her with a long, angry stride. It was Bullet Head. He caught the woman's arm and flung her violently against the paddock fence. He heard her voice faintly.

"Franz . . ."

He said something quickly, and when she shook her head, he slapped her. Durell felt a coldness creep into him that not even the heat of the sun or the rock where he sprawled could dispel. He had never felt hate like this before. In place of Cora Neville, he saw Deirdre in the hands of the

giant. His name was Franz. His name was Death. It was
eighty or ninety yards down from where Durell lay hidden
to where the big man argued with the woman. Durell's finger
tightened on the trigger of his gun. Then he forced himself
to relax. Franz pushed Cora Neville roughly toward the
house. When she stumbled and fell in the dust, he yanked
her up and flung her loosely ahead of him again. Her long
blonde hair swept wildly across her face. She stopped once
and looked back at the barn. Her hands were at her mouth,
as if to suppress horror. Franz pushed her into the house.

Durell focused on the stone barn. There was a second
floor above the stalls, with curtained windows, and he assumed there was an apartment there for the help, or perhaps for an overflow of guests. Thinking of Cora Neville's
backward glance of horror, he dismissed the main house as
a point of interest. The sunlight was blinding on the windows, and he could not see inside. Where were Miguel and
Larabee? To the south, the road wound away empty as far
as he could see. Uneasiness moved in him. Perhaps something had happened to Miguel. Perhaps he should have made
contact with Larabee himself.

He waited five more minutes.

Then he could wait no longer.

Sliding backward from the edge of the rock overhang, he
ran in a crouch toward the back of the barn, where a flight
of outside stairs led up to a landing and a door on the
second floor. Gravel slid in a small avalanche under his
feet, raising what seemed to him to be a thunderous noise.
He came up against the shadowed wall of the barn and
flattened there, the gun in his hand, waiting.

Nothing happened. There was no alarm.

Again he thought of Cora Neville's look of horror. His
mouth felt dry. He wiped his hand on his thigh and held
the gun in a lighter but firmer grip. A horse nickered in one
of the stalls. He moved on toward the neatly painted wooden
stairs that led up to the second floor.

He was on the little landing above when he heard the
sound of a car starting. He waited again, unable to see the
main house, since he faced the butte from where he had
watched before. The car drove off. He tried the door.

There was no way of telling how many hands were on the
ranch, or where they were. The door was locked. A window
next to the landing yielded to the push of his hand when

he stretched for it. Durell straddled the wooden rail, pushed the window all the way up, and spanned the distance quickly and slid inside, feet first.

A fat man in blue jeans and a flannel shirt and cowboy boots sat up sleepily from the couch across the rustic room and blinked at the gun in Durell's hand. His mouth opened. Durell hit him with the gun, heard teeth break, and hit the man again. The fat man fell over sidewise and hit the floor with a thump and was still. Blood came from his mouth and was absorbed by the braided rug. A gun had spilled from the man's belt and Durell picked it up and broke it open and pocketed the cartridges, then tossed the gun to the couch. He did everything quickly, coldly, efficiently, without a wasted motion. Every sense was keyed to a high pitch. He heard a faint sound from beyond a door across the room. This door was locked, too. He returned to the fat man, found a key ring in the man's tight jeans, picked out a likely key and tried it in the lock. There were more sounds from the next room.

When he opened the door he saw it was a bedroom, with a double-tiered Western bunk in the far corner. The room was dim with shadows, but he saw the man sprawled on the lower bunk. About twenty-eight, sandy-haired, tall, and pain-fully thin. Calvin Padgett. He knew this at once. He had seen death often enough, too, to know at once that Padgett was dead.

For the instant that he stood there, knowing now why Cora Neville had looked backward at the barn with horror, he ignored the other person in the shadowed room. Then he heard her quick intake of breath, her murmured word, and saw her move toward him.

It was Deirdre.

Chapter Thirteen . . .

Durell felt an intense relief that he had never known before. He stared at her and saw her tremulous smile. She was moving toward him and her hands came out in an appeal and he took them in his and kissed her. She was trembling violently. There was a bruise on her jaw and another on her cheek. She still wore the rust-red suit and gold blouse he had first seen her in. He could not believe that it was she, that she was here and she was alive. Yet there was no time to relish the miracle.

"How did you get here?"

"They had a plane. There's an airfield just a mile north of this place. We landed this morning. There was another girl, though—"

"Yes, she's at the Salamander."

"They wouldn't let me talk to her or warn her. And now I— Maybe I should have let them kill me," she whispered.

He followed her glance to the bunk in the corner. Durell took his hands from her and walked across the room and looked down at the dead man that every agency in the country was seeking. In death, Padgett looked young and defenseless. He had been shot twice, once in the abdomen, again through the chest. There was a lot of blood on his white shirt and on the blankets on the bunk. He felt the man's hand. It was still warm. He looked up sharply.

"When did this happen?" Durell asked.

Deirdre's lips trembled. "He came here less than an hour ago. He thought that woman, Cora Neville, would help him.

But it was a trap. I was a fool to have talked to them, thinking I could help Calvin."

Durell said, "Stop that. Nothing was your fault. It would have happened anyway." Briefly he told her about the ringer at the Salamander, and went on: "If Cal had gone there, they'd have nailed him at that plush motel. But when he got suspicious and maybe panicky, he came here, right into the lion's mouth. It was nobody's fault, Deirdre. Don't blame yourself."

She was shivering. "I can't help it. Back in Washington, the man Franz wanted to kill me, but he had orders to bring me out here. The idea was that if Calvin didn't give them what they wanted, they would torture me in front of him to make him talk." Her face was white. "When they began by slapping me, Calvin broke away and tried to fight his way out. One of the men shot him. They're all over at the ranch house now, with that woman. They'll come back soon."

"Yes. One thing, though: Did Calvin tell you why he ran away in the first place?"

She nodded and swallowed. "He was working on something. He needed a day or two to finish his calculations. That's what these people wanted from him, but he wasn't doing it for them. I—"

"Did Calvin tell you where his papers are?"

She nodded again. "In a house in Las Tiengas. It belongs to a Mexican. He left some old worthless papers in plain sight, but the real computations that meant so much to him are hidden under a loose plank in the floor by the kitchen stove."

Durell cut her off with a sharp gesture. Voices came to him from the area between the barn and the house. Quickly he moved from the bedroom and crossed the room where he had slugged the fat cowboy. There was no time even to begin to digest and evaluate the few things the girl had told him. The search for Calvin Padgett was over. The search for his work and the meaning of his work had just begun.

It looked as if he was not to be given a chance at this second quest. The voices were nearer, approaching the barn. He heard the rumble of Franz's foreign tones and Cora's low protesting voice. Another man was with them. From the doorway, Durell saw them turn the corner of the barn. He ducked back, swinging to Deirdre.

"Is there another way out of here?"

"I think there's a flight of steps down to the stables."

"Show me," he said urgently.

"But Calvin—how can we leave—"

He saw hysteria mount in her eyes, ruled by a grief that made her irrational. He slapped her face lightly. "There's nothing we can do for Calvin now."

"They killed him. They shot him down without a chance."

"Come on," he said.

They went back through the bunkroom, and she showed him a door that he thought was a closet, but which opened into a dark stairway down into the cavernous area of the barn below. Footsteps sounded on the outer steps now, coming up. It was going to be a close thing. But the sound of the others approaching snapped the irrational tension in Deirdre. She moved ahead quickly, running down the steps. Durell was close behind her. He heard the door open up there, and a sudden curse, and then he took Deirdre's hand and they ran down the aisle between the stalls, toward the big barn doors. Sunlight glared on the yard beyond. From the small door inset in the larger one, he saw that the green sedan was still parked by the main ranch house. No one else was in sight. Then a loud shout came from the apartment above the barn and was followed by a sudden thumping of feet.

Together, Durell and the girl broke from cover and sprinted across the fifty yards that separated them from the car in the driveway. They were out in the blazing open sunlight, but for the first half of the run they were sheltered by the bulk of the barn from those in the apartment above. The car was a Lancia, and Durell had driven one for a short time when he was in Europe.

A rifle cracked as Deirdre tumbled into the car and Durell spun as dirt spurted at his feet. He saw the giant, Franz, and a smaller man in a ranch hand's outfit holding a rifle. Cora Neville stood behind them at a corner of the barn. Durell snapped a shot that made the trio duck back for cover and then he jumped into the Lancia. He had the motor started when the rifle cracked again and glass shattered in the back.

The rear wheels spun and the car lurched ahead. He twisted down the driveway, gained a momentary respite as the ranch house intervened between the road and the barn. The rifle cracked again. He did not look back. He felt the car bounce wildly and it slued at the first turn that curved to the valley floor, but it held the road. Deirdre kept looking back through the broken rear window. Durell checked the gas gauge. There was enough. The desert highway stretched ahead, with no other cars in sight anywhere in the barren waste.

"They're not following us," Deirdre breathed.

"No. They'll have to pull out of there now. All of them. They'll have to run for cover."

He was still not over his relief at finding Deirdre alive. Now he thought of Miguel, and Larabee's failure to appear. Something had gone wrong. But was it with Miguel or with Larabee? Dickinson McFee had been uneasy about the personnel at the Las Tiengas Base. McFee had told him not to trust anyone here. Larabee was hostile. And John Padgett, the broken eagle, the man in charge of everything? Padgett was hostile, too, making it plain he felt his brother must have been guilty of subversion. But Calvin was dead now. That part was over.

Yet he still felt that something was deadly wrong.

It was not quite four o'clock when Durell turned the Lancia into the street where Miguel lived. From the old Spanish church nearby came the dolorous clangor of iron bells, heavy in the afternoon heat. He parked the car near the corner and looked at the little Mexican fruit store across the street. Several people stood there, and included in the group was a black-garbed priest. Durell told Deirdre to stay in the car and then walked across the street to join the people in the shade of the awning. He looked back at Miguel's house, but the door was closed and it looked normal. He imagined that Franz and Cora Neville and Weederman were already flying from the ranch for the border. They were of less importance than what had to be done here.

The people outside the store were talking in Spanish. When the priest moved aside as Durell approached, a wide irregular stain was visible on the sidewalk.

Their eyes were flat and opaque, sensing he was a stranger. Only the priest seemed friendly. Durell spoke in Spanish. "Forgive me for disturbing you, but can you tell me what happened here?"

"A man was killed," said the priest.

"Some *pistoleros* shot him down," said a stout woman angrily.

"Miguel?" Durell asked.

"Ah. Did you know Miguel Santos?"

"We were friends," Durell said. "I am shocked and sorry."

"He is in the arms of God," said the priest.

"That is certain." Durell nodded. "Did anyone see the killers?"

"No one. Paco was inside. Then the shots came just as Miguel was entering the store. He had a coin in his hand. It is a great tragedy and an even greater mystery. Miguel never harmed anyone. He was a good man. Why should anyone desire his death?"

"What did the police say?"

The priest looked pained. "The police of Las Tiengas are not concerned with the death of a Mexican. I do not say this in anger, but in sorrow. They consider it as a feud between strangers. But who could hold death in his heart for such as Miguel?"

Durell returned to the green Lancia across the street. He knew now why Larabee had never come to Cora Neville's ranch. Life was cheap for those who had followed him and Miguel from the Salamander. They must have shot down the old man within moments after Durell had left to recover his car. He had not heard the shots because the bulk of the old mission church had intervened, muffling the sound.

Deirdre saw his face and said, "What's the matter, Sam? What happened?"

He told her bluntly, hoping it would help her to see her brother's death against the background of those they were fighting. She got out of the car and stood on the hot, sunny sidewalk with him. The group at the corner still stood there, and entry into Miguel's house from the front was out of the question.

Durell took the girl's arm. The priest was watching as they turned the corner and walked around the block. He felt uneasy about leaving the green sedan so prominently exposed on the street, but there was no help for it. He did not think West, or Weederman, would have anything on his mind except flight, with Calvin dead and Deirdre lost to them.

A narrow alley led them to the back door of Miguel's house. The lock to the little fenced yard was flimsy, yielding when Durell hit it sharply with his gun. He followed Deirdre across a neat little patio and then into the tiny house.

There were signs of disturbance that showed a search had been made, but nothing else. Durell went toward the old-fashioned iron stove and studied the floor boards for a moment, then used a kitchen knife to pry up the board he selected. It came up easily. Underneath was a sheaf of yellow pages, perhaps a dozen in all, every one covered with neat formulae, computations, equations. He turned them over and over in his hands. They meant nothing to him. Yet they could mean everything to someone who knew what they were all about.

Deirdre stood quietly with her hands at her sides, not looking at him. Durell found a bottle of red wine, uncorked it, and poured some into two glasses and handed one to the girl. She took it mechanically.

"Drink some," Durell said. "You need it. If you're thinking of Cal, you can still help him. You can tell me everything he said to you. Everything that happened since they snatched you away from my apartment in Washington."

She looked at him. "I thought that was a trap. I didn't trust you then, Sam. I acted like a fool and spoiled everything."

"It was a natural reaction. But I hope you trust me now."

"I do." She nodded slowly. "I wasn't going to tell them anything about my arrangement to meet Cal at the Salamander. Not at first. Franz was horrible. He was going to kill me. Then I thought that I had told you about the Salamander and I knew you would come here and I hoped that if I told them about it, you would be here to get them."

"Did Franz hurt you?"

"Not too much. They kept me in an empty house for that evening, then they blindfolded me and drove me out of the city to a farm, where there was a private plane. The other girl was there. She looked like me and I understood she was going to pretend to be me. Franz wanted to kill me then. There was a big argument and finally they telephoned to Las Tiengas and I guess they were ordered to bring me along to make Cal talk if the ruse with the other girl didn't succeed. Today, when Cal showed up at the ranch, he thought the Neville woman was his friend. She didn't like any of this, but I think George West has some hold over her. He made her obey him."

Durell nodded. "Yes, I gathered that much."

"When Cal saw me, tied and gagged, he almost broke down. Then they left us alone and he told me why he ran away from the base."

Durell waited. The girl walked around the room, holding the wineglass in both hands. Her face was pale. When Durell looked at her, he wanted to hold her and protect her against everyone in the world. The house was quiet. Then Deirdre turned to him and he saw a new look of determination and anger in her face, and it made him feel even better about her.

"Cal ran away from the base because he felt there was a plot to sabotage Cyclops and he wanted time to prove he was right. No one listened to him. He had the job only because John vouched for him and accepted responsibility for his security. John wouldn't listen, or Larabee, or General Aiken, when Calvin insisted that the launching of Cyclops should be delayed."

Durell nodded. "In what way was Cyclops to be sabotaged?"

"In the calculations that set the orbit, in what he called the brain. I couldn't understand it all," the girl said slowly. She bit her lower lip. "Some of the equations were juggled so that Cyclops, instead of breaking free of gravity, would traverse an arc and land somewhere in the eastern United States. He was terribly worried over it. He wanted to use the electronic computers to prove his case, but Larabee and General Aiken refused, and even John backed them up. Finally they decided he was suffering a nervous breakdown. That was the mild way they let him know they no longer considered him responsible."

"You knew Cal best," Durell said. "How was he?"

"Perfectly normal. Upset and worried, yes. He was afraid of what will happen when they fire Cyclops. He spent two days without sleep, computing manually the equations that would have taken only a few minutes on the electronic calculators. He proved to himself he was right."

"And he told you all this in that barn?"

Deirdre nodded. Her anger helped her recover somewhat from the shock of her brother's death. "Calvin didn't tell the woman or Franz anything, not even when they threatened to torture me. He was not a traitor. And I think he was right. Cyclops *has* been sabotaged."

"And these papers can prove it?"

"That's what he said."

Durell lit a cigarette. He believed Deirdre. Calvin had not been a traitor. But there was a traitor at the base, someone high up in power, with the authority to quash Calvin Padgett's protests and have him committed to the solitude of a hospital cell. Dickinson McFee, as far away as Washington, had sensed something wrong at Las Tiengas. Durell felt a sudden danger in the possession of Padgett's calculations. Somebody had to check them before Cyclops was launched. As far as Weederman's apparatus was concerned, their mission would be fulfilled if Padgett's work went ignored. Durell was suddenly sure that they must have somehow found out about Padgett's suspicions. So they might assume the existence of these papers and these explosive equations. They would stop at nothing to destroy them, to have the sabotage attempt succeed.

The silence in the little house was suddenly thick with tension. Durell started to fold the papers and put them away. And an angry voice spoke from the doorway:

"Hold it like that. What in hell do you think you've been doing today, Durell?"

It was Colonel Larabee. John Padgett stood behind him, leaning heavily on his knobby walking stick, his head thrust forward. Larabee had a service Colt in his hand and it was pointed at Durell's stomach.

John Padgett said mildly, "Deirdre, my dear, whatever are you doing in Las Tiengas?"

The girl looked at her older brother with nothing in her eyes at all, as if he were a stranger. She moved closer to Durell.

"Calvin is dead," she whispered.

"You found him?" Larabee asked sharply.

She nodded. Durell said, "How did you locate us, Mike?"

Larabee looked even angrier. "I just got the report on the little Mex shot down at the corner. It coupled up with the business of Cora Neville and the Salamander. Professor Padgett happened to be with me and we came to take a look. What's going on?"

Durell told him. He made it brief and succinct, wondering if this was a mistake, but seeing no choice with Larabee's gun probing his middle. He watched John Padgett as he spoke. The man's gaunt, predatory face was puzzled, then smooth and gently smiling. He made no gesture of affection

toward Deirdre. When Durell stopped speaking, Padgett said
quietly, "And those are poor Calvin's calculations?"

"They are." Durell nodded. "They should be checked."

"Nonsense. Calvin was not in his right mind. Getting
mixed up with a bunch of spies is ridiculous on the face of
it. I think your story is nonsense. I don't even believe he's
dead. And certainly those equations aren't worth the paper
they're written on."

"What makes you so sure?" Durell asked.

"I humored Calvin at first. We went over the problem
together. He's lost his capacity for logical thinking."

Durell swung to Larabee. "Take that gun off me, Mike."

"I'm taking you into custody. I spoke to Swayney this
noon about you. He says you've lost your head over this
girl. He says you're not to be trusted. That's a pretty cock-
and-bull story about Cora Neville and this Weederman, but
Swayney says Weederman was executed a couple of years
ago in the Soviet Zone of Austria, as a neo-Nazi. And Cora
Neville is vouched for by very high sources. She couldn't be
a Red or work with the Reds. Until we check out what
you've told us, you're under arrest, Durell. The girl, too."

John Padgett picked up the pages of equations and was
crumpling them, smiling, ready to put them to flame in the
kerosene stove. In the moment's silence, Durell weighed his
move swiftly. He heard Deirdre suck in an angry breath.
Durell said, "One thing, Mike. Before you let Professor
Padgett destroy those equations, let me call Dickinson Mc-
Fee in Washington. General McFee has over-all command
over the hardware being built here. Let's hear what he
says about this. Telephone him now."

John Padgett went on crumpling the papers. Larabee
shook his head. "I'm in command here. McFee wouldn't
know anything about this. I reported to Swayney, and he
told me what to do."

"Please," Durell said. "Call McFee."

"To hell with you," said Larabee.

But his glance shifted with momentary unease toward the
gaunt figure of John Padgett at the stove. Durell had no
choice. A match scratched and flared as Padgett crumpled
more of the paper. Then Durell swung at Larabee's gun with
his left, knocked it down, and hit Larabee's bulldog jaw with
his right. The gun went off with a shattering crash, spanking
a bullet into the floor. Larabee's eyes glazed and Durell hit

him again. The gun fell and Larabee slammed into the wall, shaking the little house. Durell swung toward Padgett, snatched the papers from the flame, and shook off a charred corner. The gaunt man's face was yellow. His angry eyes touched Larabee, then Durell.

"You must be insane! You will regret this."

Durell scooped up Larabee's gun. "Get away from that stove." He squashed the papers into his pocket, jamming them securely, glanced at Deirdre. She had not moved. The echoes of Larabee's single shot still vibrated in the air.

Larabee was reviving. He sat up. His eyes fixed on Durell with hatred. "I'll fix you. I told you I didn't like prima donnas. You've gone haywire. What in hell do you think you're doing? You'll rot in a federal pen when I'm through with you!"

"Get up," Durell said.

Larabee started up slowly, then suddenly lunged in a low charge. Durell caught his chin with a sharply lifted knee. Larabee's head snapped back, his eyes rolled up, and he fell over heavily. Durell weighed the gun and looked at John Padgett. The other hadn't moved.

"Deirdre, come along," Durell said.

"Don't go with him," Padgett said. "He's a madman."

Durell would have felt better with Professor Padgett on the floor beside Larabee. But the man didn't move and he couldn't do anything about it. He took Deirdre's hand and she went with him without a backward glance.

They ran down into the narrow street, in the hot afternoon sun. How much time did he have? Five minutes. Maybe ten. Then every cop in town would be alerted for him. He had no illusions about Larabee. Larabee would never forgive him.

Deirdre ran with him until they passed the old mission church. There were people here on the sidewalk, and Durell slowed to a walk. Deirdre breathed with difficulty. He kept looking for a telephone as they walked toward the center of town. But because he needed one, because it was imperative to get on a line to Dickinson McFee before they were picked up, he couldn't find a public booth. As they neared Cactus Street, he heard the wail of sirens behind them.

Chapter Fourteen . . .

The bar was named the Lucky Dollar, and there was a huge neon sign in the window, formed as a silver cartwheel. Inside, it was cool and air-conditioned, with dark oak booths and a long bar glimmering with dim lights behind the racked tiers of bottles. Music played softly somewhere. There were only a few customers. The long blinds in the window were tilted to shut out the hot glare of the sun. They also shut out the sight of traffic and pedestrians on Cactus Street.

Durell ordered beer and sandwiches and counted his money. Ninety-two dollars. Deirdre had no handbag. She was trying to straighten her copper hair with her hands. Even without lipstick or make-up, she looked wonderful. Durell got some change and went into the phone booth at the back end of the bar. A siren screamed past outside.

He got the operator, asked for long-distance. Sweat rolled down under his shirt. The receiver hummed. He wanted to jiggle the hook, but he waited. Finally the operator came on and he gave Dickinson McFee's private number in Washington, D.C. The operator asked him to wait. He waited.

He could hear the phone ringing two thirds of the way across the continent. The operator asked for money, and he dropped coins into the slot in a steady stream.

There was no answer.

The operator said, "I'll try again in twenty minutes."

"No, wait," Durell said. "There's got to be an answer."

"I'm sor-ry. I'll try again in—"

"Wait." He gave Swayney's number at 20 Annapolis Street. The booth was suffocating. There were clicks and buzzes on the line. Where in hell was McFee? Out of his office, maybe in conference somewhere. Just when you needed him. He hated to talk to Swayney. The phone began to ring again,

and when he shifted his weight in the narrow booth, he felt
Calvin Padgett's papers crackle thickly in his pocket.

The phone went dead. He jiggled the hook.

"Operator, what's the matter?"

"I'm sor-ry, the circuits are busy. I'll try again—"

"Never mind."

He hung up and left the booth. Their sandwiches and
beer were on the table as he slid to the seat across from
Deirdre. Her mouth was tense. "Did you get McFee?"

"No answer, busy circuits. It's a clutch. And every minute
Larabee gets more and more stacked off."

"What will we do?"

"Try to keep out of Larabee's hands until I get McFee."

"In this town?"

"I've got to try," Durell said. "Your brother wants to destroy these papers." He looked at her. Her eyes were pained.
"You didn't tell me everything, did you?"

"No," she whispered.

"You didn't tell me about John."

"No."

"Eat your sandwich," Durell said.

"I can't."

"Then pretend to. Calvin didn't trust John, did he? It was
John who balked him, who put a bug in the medico's ear
about Calvin being off his rocker. That right?"

"Yes."

"John designed Cyclops, but he's going to sabotage it.
That right, too?"

"Yes. That's what Calvin thought. He was sure of it. But
he didn't want to do anything until he spoke to me. After
all, our own brother—"

"He's our enemy."

"I'm afraid of him," Deirdre said.

"His word is law at the base. What he says goes. We
can't argue with anyone here if John says no. It will be
different when I get in touch with McFee."

Another siren went past the bar. Durell drank his beer.
It tasted sour. He saw Dierdre's hands tremble on the table.
He didn't know what to do. He wanted to try the telephone
booth again, but it was too soon. Maybe it had been a mistake to slug Larabee. But he couldn't have let John Padgett
burn those papers. No use crying about that. It was done,
finished.

Deirdre was looking at a man at the far end of the bar. Her gray eyes were shadowed with sudden fear. Her hand touched his.

"Sam?"

"Take it easy. What is it?"

"There is the pilot."

"What pilot?"

"The man who flew the plane that took me out here."

"Has he seen you?"

"Yes, I think so."

Durell looked at the man at the bar. Tall, thin, cropped yellow hair, a sunburned face, big freckles. He looked very drunk. His eyes were owlish. Not dangerous. He wore a yellow sport shirt hanging loose over his slacks. When his eyes met Durell's he grinned easily and picked up his drink and walked toward the booth. His gait wavered. He winked at Deirdre and lurched into a seat.

"Hi, baby. I never thought I'd see you again! How come those s.o.b.'s let you run around loose?"

Durell had his hand in his pocket on his gun, but suddenly he did not think he needed it. This man was very drunk. He also sensed a depth of relief in him because he saw Deirdre alive, and this apparently satisfied and gratified the pilot.

"I tell you," said the man, shaking his blond head. "When I heard them shots in the barn, I cut loose. I don't want no part of it, I tell me. I'm glad they didn't hurt you, baby. They're a crazy crowd."

"How come you work for them?" Durell asked quietly.

"They got me where it hurts. They got ol' Tex Feener all tied up in knots. I don't mean I gotta believe the crap they hand me. All I believe is what will happen to Willie if I don't fly 'em here and there when they ask me to."

"Who is Willie?"

"The kid brother. The Chinese Reds are holdin' him prisoner. He was 'chuted down for a look-see for the Formosa people, and he got rapped. They want to shoot him, but this crowd says no as long as I'm a good boy. You think I talk too much, chum?"

"Talk some more. You mean you work for Weederman and Franz only because they've sewn up your brother?"

"Check. The dirty bastards. But I'm sure glad they didn't hurt this li'l gal. I hauled tail outa that ranch house fast."

Durell remembered having heard a car leave Cora Neville's house while he was investigating the barn. He looked at Feener and felt he had something in the man if he handled it right.

"How drunk are you?"

Feener grinned loosely. "Pretty damned drunk."

"Can you fly a plane?"

"Hell, that's when I'm best."

"Would you fly us somewhere?" Durell asked.

Feener stopped grinning. "No."

"Do they know you're here in town, drinking?"

"Hell, no."

"Suppose you get picked up by the cops? You've got a loose mouth, Feener. You could talk a lot. You could do Uncle Sam a lot of good. Maybe you could help Willie more if you helped us."

"Are you a cop?" Feener was shocked. Suddenly he looked less drunk than before. He lurched up, but Durell caught his arm and held him in the seat.

"There's nothing to be afraid of," Durell told him.

"They'll kill me," Feener whispered.

"Wouldn't you like to help yourself and your brother and be rid of them for good?"

"They'll kill Willie."

"Do you really think he's still alive?"

"I can't take the chance he's not."

"These people don't value anyone's life highly," Durell said. "Those shots you heard weren't just to scare Dierdre. They killed her brother with those shots. They'll kill you just for talking to me. Do you understand what I'm saying, or are you still too drunk?"

Feener's eyes shifted from Durell to the girl. He looked young and helpless. "I don't know what to do."

Durell said, "Listen to me. We've got to get out of Las Tiengas. Will you help us that far?"

"Are they after you, too?"

"I've got to contact my boss in Washington. You can believe me when I say it's important. You know something big is cooking here, or the crowd you've been working for wouldn't be so jacked up, right?"

"Yeah. It's something big."

"Big enough to wreck the country," Durell said. "You were in Korea, weren't you?"

"Two years."

"That was duck soup. That was nothing to what will happen if Weederman gets me or the girl. And we can't trust the cops here in Las Tiengas. Have you got a car?"

"The one I came in. It's parked up the street."

"Are you sober enough to drive?"

"I reckon so."

"Let's go get it," Durell said.

Feener didn't move. His eyes looked at something far away. He drew a deep, shuddering breath. He started to lift his drink and put it down again. He looked at Deirdre.

"I'm glad you're alive, baby. I'll do it for you."

The field was a level green pasture, cropped smooth, with low fences and a barn that served as a hangar. The twin-motored cabin plane was parked in front of the wide doors. Bees hummed and sang in the clover. The sky to the west was bloody with a violent sunset. It had taken less than twenty minutes to cover the twenty miles north out of town in the station wagon Feener had produced. By now, Durell knew, the roadblocks were up, scout cars patrolled the highways, MP's were checking every bar, every hotel, every house in town. He knew the kind of man Larabee was. Thorough, patient, implacable.

It was five-thirty in the afternoon.

Feener showed him where the telephone was in the hangar. There was no one else at the field. While he waited for the long-distance operator, he said, "Feener, is that your own plane?"

Feener nodded. "They've got a whole network of private fields and planes. You got no idea. The organization doesn't miss much."

"Where has Weederman gone?"

"I wouldn't know. Anywhere. He's smart and tricky."

The operator sang her singsong and Durell gave Dickinson McFee's number again. The phone buzzed, clicked, hummed. It was hot inside the hangar. Deirdre stood in the wide doorway, watching the field. The telephone rang and rang. Durell sweated.

There was no answer.

He jiggled the hook and gave the operator his own office number. The operator sounded odd. There was a lot of noise on the line. Then Hazel Getcher, his secretary. He relaxed when he heard her voice.

"Hazel, this is Sam."

"Oh, Lordie!"

"Where in hell is Dickinson McFee?"

"Sam, get off the line."

"I've got to reach McFee."

"He's at the Pentagon. Everything broke loose. What have you done? No, don't tell me. Just hang up."

"I've got to talk to McFee."

Another voice, Burritt Swayney. "Durell, where are you?"

Durell drew a deep breath. "Burritt, Padgett is dead."

"No, he isn't. I just spoke to him."

"You spoke to John."

"You mean Calvin is dead?"

"I've got what he was working on. I've got to get it to McFee."

Swayney's voice was suddenly too calm, too friendly. "All right, Sam. That's fine. You've done a good job. But what did you slug Larabee for? The wires have been melting for ten minutes. Look, you stay where you are. Larabee will come for you and—"

"Nobody comes for me," Durell said. "I want to talk to McFee."

"Over my head?"

"McFee sent me out here."

"You son-of-a-bitch, you've caused enough trouble. You stay where you are and—"

Durell hung up.

It was an effort to move.

But he had to move. He had to get away fast. He knew the call was being traced. Larabee would be here in minutes.

"Feener?"

"Yeah. No dice, huh?"

"Is there gas in that plane?"

"I topped the tanks myself."

"Can you fly?"

"I'm O.K. now."

"Then let's go."

"Anyplace in particular?"

"Away from here. East."

Durell took Dierdre's hand and they ran for the plane.

Chapter Fifteen . . .

East into the darkening purple of evening. Over long shadows, down the narrow slots of violent canyons to avoid the high screaming shadows of jet eagles combing the desert. Here and there a light twinkled. Then other lights and it was dark, complete night, and the plane lifted, free of the need to hug the ground and skim the hills to avoid being seen. They soared. They rose higher toward the stars, the full moon. The hours and the miles passed.

The plane seated four and the pilot. Feener's head was bent forward a little at the controls, his face reflected from the glass and the dim glow of the instruments. The twin motors sang steadily with power. Durell sat with Deirdre. She was asleep, her hand trustingly in his.

Feener took the radio earphones from his head. He twisted to meet Durell's glance.

"They're looking for you, all right."

"Where are they looking?"

"Everywhere. The air is full of it."

"Do they know about the plane?"

"Not yet, but they will. We'll have to refuel somewhere."

"How much longer can we go?"

"Couple of hours. There's a mess up ahead, too. Over Texas. A storm coming in from the Gulf."

"Can we skirt it?"

"We can sneak in behind it. Cut south, get on its tail."

"All right," Durell said. "You're flying this ship."

"I ought to have my head examined." Feener sighed. "I don't know what I'm doing. I don't know anything about you. If I hadn't been lapping it up, this wouldn't have happened. You know what? I'm scared. I'm chicken down to my toes. I don't want to listen to the radio no more. We put down at any public field, they're waiting with guns."

"It's that bad?"

"I never heard anything like it," Feener said.

The winds picked them up, bounced them, grew turbulent with a playfulness that held menace in its strength. Deirdre was awake. He sat beside her, still held her hand. When he looked at her, she smiled.

"Are you all right?" he asked.

"All right now."

Feener was singing softly to himself. He had to pay constant attention to the controls. The lights of earth were blotted out and rain hammered at the cabin windows. The plane tossed, fell, lifted, slued. The rain grew heavier.

"Half an hour," Feener said. "There's Marysville."

"Are they waiting for us there?"

"They're waiting everywhere."

Durell thought of something. "You said Weederman's crowd had a network of private fields they used for courier work. Is there one near here?"

Feener said harshly, "You want to take your chances with *them* instead of the cops?"

"Who would be at the nearest field?"

"Fellow I know. Crop-duster."

"Is he like you? Is he with them willingly, or because they have something on him?"

"I don't know. We never talked about it. They pay good, y'know? Real good. And if they got something on you, you keep your mouth shut and kid yourself that it's just another flying job. Maybe you don't sleep so good, but what's a man to do? We land at Olsen's, we take the chance he keeps his mouth shut."

"It's better than Marysville," Durell decided.

The plane banked, swung farther south toward the Gulf coast. They had been flying for almost six hours. Durell tried to fight off the feeling of being trapped. Up here in the plane in the black, turbulent night, he felt helpless to do what had to be done. McFee had to be warned without delay. There was time enough to reach the general and stop the launching of Cyclops. But there was John Padgett in control of the Las Tiengas Base, swaying Larabee and the commanding officers. Durell felt frustrated. John Padgett was the traitor, not Calvin. But was Padgett involved with the Weederman apparatus? There had been no hint of it.

"Deirdre."

She looked at him calmly. "Yes?"

"About John. Did Calvin say who he was working with, or why John was sabotaging Cyclops?"

"John wasn't working with anyone."

"Then why is he destroying it?"

"Calvin thought it was John who joined all those subversive outfits in the past. We didn't have much time to talk about it, but Calvin thought John had used his name, Calvin's, when he signed up with them. He couldn't think of any other way it could have happened."

"Then John *is* working for Weederman."

She shook her head. "John is strange. He could be doing this out of a sense of grievance against the world, because he was crippled, because of our parents. . . . I just don't know."

"He could sell us out by giving every detail about Cyclops to Weederman," Durell said heavily.

"No. John's ego is enormous. He'd do this alone, or not at all."

"I hope you're right," Durell said.

The plane went into a sharp bank. Through the cabin window he glimpsed the dark loom of earth a thousand feet below. The rain had slackened. Here and there a light twinkled as the plane lost altitude. There was a change in the set of Feener's head and shoulders as he leaned forward in the pilot's seat, a quick and competent tension in the way he held himself. The plane circled twice. The earth was a great dark pit below, waiting to receive them.

Feener gave a long sigh as lights suddenly flared. He banked again and the plane jolted and Deirdre's fingers closed on Durell's wrist. Her hand was cold. The plane jolted again and dropped and something black flashed past the window. A tree. And another. The plane bumped, bounced, settled down. The cabin rocked wildly. For several moments they rushed over a rough field as if hurtling headlong to destruction. Then Feener grunted and pulled down the tail and the brakes squealed and the plane came to rest.

For a moment nobody spoke. The warm smell of plowed earth mingled curiously with the salt of the sea. The rain made a soft, gentle pattering sound on the metal wings.

"This is Olsen's place," Feener said. "Be careful what you say to him."

He got out and Deirdre jumped down and Durell joined them. Floodlights glared and he heard the sound of a wet wind and he saw the dim bulk of a barn and a house beyond the blazing light. It was just ten o'clock. Feener strode toward a man who came at them in a jeep.

Olsen, introduced by Feener, looked at them with flat, opaque eyes that gave nothing away. He was burly, in his forties, with a sullen mouth and a grudging air. His hair was thin and straggly. He wore a white shirt open at the collar and slacks stuffed into ornate red boots. Durell asked if he could use the phone while the plane was being refueled.

"In the house, mister. I'll show you."

There was a woman in the house who looked timidly at Durell and hovered in the hallway. Olsen spoke angrily and she vanished. The house was drab and unkempt. As Durell picked up the phone, Olsen said, "You a friend of Feener's?"

"Yes."

"Courier?"

Durell looked at him. "Do you really want to know?"

Olsen was immediately defensive. "It ain't that I'm curious, mister. You just gotta be careful, is all." He had a thick Texas drawl. "Go ahead and use the phone. It ain't tapped."

"Help Feener with the gas," Durell said, putting command into his voice.

"All right. Don't get sore."

"Then don't get nosy."

Olsen went out. Durell asked the operator for Hazel Getcher's home number, and this time there was no difficulty. His ring was answered at once, as if she had been waiting for him.

"Hazel," he said, "were you able to get in touch with McFee?"

"Oh, Lordie. I can't. He's in New York, Sam."

"When will he be back?"

"Tomorrow. Are you all right?"

"So far."

"Swayney has blown all his fuses. He thinks you sold out for the girl. He says Calvin Padgett was a traitor."

"That's all wrong," Durell said. "You believe me, don't you?"

"Of course. But what are you going to do?"

"I'm heading for home. I'll have to see McFee personally.

But there isn't much time. Keep trying to contact him, will you? The project has to be delayed. No fireworks for the Fourth, do you understand?"

"I've got it, but—"

The phone clicked sharply.

There was a brief silence.

"Did you hear that, Sam?" Hazel asked.

"You're being tapped. So long."

"Oh, Lordie. They'll trace you."

"I won't be here more than five minutes."

He hung up. He was sweating again as he returned to the plane.

Flight.

Deirdre slept. She looked sweet and tired and defenseless. Durell fretted. He watched Feener put on the headphones and listen intently, and he moved forward to join the pilot.

"What does it sound like?"

Feener shook his head. "Not good. The weather front runs west to east, just north of us. Pretty clear all along the Gulf coast, though."

"Are they still looking for us?"

"More than before," Feener said, nodding.

"What about that Olsen? Do you trust him?"

"He asked a lot of questions I didn't like. No, I'd say I don't trust him."

"Is he apt to check on you?"

"Could be. Where are we headed for now, Mr. Durell?"

Durell thought about it. "You're heading for the Delta, right? Is there another field like Olsen's there?"

Feener consulted a map spread on his thin knees. "About thirty miles south of New Orleans. It's only three hours away. A guy named Jamie runs a charter service there. I don't know him."

"We'll put down there. Maybe by then we can cut north."

"I've been thinking about Willie, Mr. Durell."

"You're doing the right thing," Durell said.

"I dunno. I mean, maybe they shot him long ago. He was doing a job and doing it right. Maybe he wouldn't have wanted me to work with these people like I did. But suppose they kill him because of tonight?"

"He knew the risk when he dropped into China."

"Yeah. He was crazy for it." Feener bit his lip. "The port engine don't sound so good. Maybe we better try

Jamie's, at that. And maybe I belong in a federal pen. Maybe they'll really ream me when this is all over."

"I'll take care of that. Let's try for Jamie's field."

Durell got up and went back to the seat beside Deirdre. She was awake. Her gray eyes were clear and warm. She smiled and turned to face him and looked at him with an intent gravity.

"What is it?" he asked.

"Nothing. Everything."

"Riddles?"

"I feel good. Why should I feel good? Calvin is dead and we're in terrible trouble. But somehow I feel it will be all right."

"You know what your brother John is, don't you?"

"He's like a stranger. Yes, I know."

"Will you help me turn him in?"

"Yes. For Calvin's sake." She paused. "I don't want to talk about it. I've been thinking of you. The way you looked when you saw me in that barn. When you first came in, you looked terrible. It was frightening. Then you saw me and you changed."

"I was worried about you. I thought they had killed you."

"And it mattered that much?"

"That's a leading question."

"I feel as if I've known you forever, Sam. It's strange. There was a boy, once. He was killed in Korea. I never stopped thinking about him, and I didn't want any more of that. It hurt too much when I lost him. It was a nightmare. But now I feel better about it. You made me feel better. I think I was turning into a spinster and rejecting the world, and now I don't feel like a spinster at all." She looked away from him and flushed. "Do you understand?"

"Yes."

"Do you feel it, too?"

"Yes."

"Say it, Sam."

"No."

She kissed him. Her mouth was soft and fragile and warm and clinging. "I don't care. I saw how you looked at me in that barn. It's enough for now."

He could not bring himself to say anything.

Chapter Sixteen . . .

There was no rain now, but Feener had trouble locating the field. The port engine was erratic. Twice he swept down the torrential reach of the Mississippi, checking landmarks, his young freckled face one vast scowl as he consulted the map on his knee. Durell tried to remember when he had been back to the bayous last. Four years? Maybe five. No matter. It was after midnight, and the third of July had begun.

Lights flickered at last to the left, a definite pattern that blinked twice and then shone steadily. Feener banked the plane that way. He looked worried. He circled several times. He shook his head. "We got another two hours' fuel. You think we ought to try this, Mr. Durell? I don't know this Jamie. I don't like the way Olsen acted. But that port motor needs looking at."

"We might as well find out the worst right now," Durell said.

The port motor banged and shot out a streamer of flame and Feener suddenly snapped off switches with quick, precise motions. His face was white. The flame spurted farther toward the tail, then abruptly died. The prop stopped spinning. The plane dipped, slued, steadied on one engine.

"No choice," Feener said.

"Let's go down. We're lucky."

They landed smoothly. The field was simply a cleared area on the edge of a dark bayou, surrounded by towering live oaks and water on three sides. There was no hangar. To the left, dimly visible under the makeshift field lights, was a fishing camp of half a dozen rickety shacks, with a pier and several pirogues tied up to the shore. The night was thick with humid heat. The familiar noises of swamp and bayou edged in upon the sluggish air when Feener cut the motor.

Nobody came to greet them.

The floodlights blinked and went out. Darkness swooped over the field except for the dim lights shining in one wooden shack that was larger than the others, presumably the proprietor's house. Feener got out of the plane and Durell helped Deirdre down. Something splashed in the bayou fifty feet away. The Spanish moss on the oaks made a dark, heavy curtain all around them. There was a smell of mud and decay and stagnant water in the torpid air.

The field was empty, dark. Metal cooled on the plane with sharp crackling noises. Nobody showed up.

"You better stay here while I look," Feener muttered.

The pilot walked toward the lighted cabin before Durell could object. His thin figure was briefly outlined against the rectangle of an open doorway, then was gone.

Durell waited.

The bayou chuckled, groaned, clacked, gurgled.

The single shot ripped everything apart.

It was followed by a high thin scream, and then Feener's shout. "Run! That bastard Olsen—"

Durell grabbed Deirdre's hand and they ran. He had no choice of direction. They ran toward the black, glimmering edge of the bayou. Two shots slammed after them. Nothing came near. Then another. Durell heard the whine and slap of air against his head as if someone had boxed his ear, and he grabbed Deirdre and slid recklessly down the embankment toward the dock where the pirogues were tied up. Someone shouted from the cabins. Durell looked at Deirdre's startled white face. "All right?"

She nodded. "Yes."

"Get in the pirogue."

"But Feener—"

"Gone. Get in!" he said harshly.

She moved carefully onto the rickety dock. Footsteps grated, pounded across the field toward the edge of the *chenière*. Quick, careful, crafty. Durell tried to guess how many men there were. Four. Maybe five. He had his gun ready, but the three shots that had slammed after them came from a rifle. He thought of Olsen's hostile attitude. The network had been alerted to look for them. He made himself breathe deeply and regularly. He listened. There were soft whisperings, a curse, a muffled order.

"Durell!"

A strange voice, harsh in the still swamp, shattering the hot dark night. The pirogue bumped the sagging dock behind him, but he did not look back at Deirdre.

"Come out of there, Durell! We can talk business!"

He felt a moment's despair. He had covered more than a thousand miles, but the telephone wires had sung their siren warning far ahead of him. Soft laughter came from the shadowed field. Abruptly the rifle crashed and mud jumped only inches from his leg. Deirdre called softly from the pirogue. Durell slid down to the dock and ran along it as she pulled the narrow boat into the reeds along shore. The pirogue rocked perilously as he threw himself in. A handgun crashed, and water stung his face. Then he had a paddle in his hand and he drove the needleshaped craft hard, with competent, remembered strokes, through the reeds parallel to the embankment. Clearing the dock, he saw the knees of old cypress trees and swung that way, and when the ghostly roots formed a web around him he picked up his gun and looked back. A dim shape stood on the dock, rifle leveled. He fired. The man screamed and fell into the water.

Deirdre whispered, "No, Sam. No!"

"They want to kill us," he grated. The words were rust in his throat. Blood hammered in him. The pirogue floated easily among the massive cypress roots. They thrust up from the black water like drowning hands.

Her voice was calm. "Do you know where we are?"

"A rough idea. Not far from where I was raised. Twenty miles, perhaps."

"We'll have to hide for the night. There's nothing else we can do. Tomorrow we can figure out what to do."

He looked at her gratefully. She was calm. She gave him a steadying strength. When he picked up the paddle, she leaned toward him in the pirogue, smiling, and her lips brushed his.

"I love you, Sam."

He had been paddling for only a few minutes when he heard the motorboat behind them. The channel was choked with reeds, overhung with moss that trailed on the surface of the water. The tortuous passage twisted away from the narrow end of the bayou. Insects sang, hummed, fed upon them. The pulse of the boat motor wakened flat echoes through the hot, misted darkness. Now the quick flicker of a spotlight probed the swamp. It passed overhead and sliced through the trees and the black shapes of three sleeping buzzards stirred and took off with a giant thrashing of angry wings. Deirdre shuddered. Durell drove the pirogue ahead with hard strokes. Sweat ran down his face and down his chest and belly.

Light suddenly flickered on the water beside them, and a man shouted. A narrow opening appeared to the right and Durell took the chance that the watery slot was not a dead end. He twisted the boat into it. Foliage and moss fell like a curtain behind them.

The narrow channel widened into a shallow pond where even the pirogue scraped bottom. Water hyacinth choked the way and Deirdre leaned forward over the prow and tore the vegetation aside with her hands. It was hard, sweaty, gasping work. It was incredibly hot. The pond yielded to another channel, another slough, another pond. Durell looked back. The light was gone. The beat of the motor was only a faint pulse through the dark mist. He stopped paddling.

"We'd better rest. They can't follow us now."

Without the faint stir of air created by their passage, the heat closed in like a heavy fog. Durell looked at the luminous dial of his watch. It was two o'clock in the morning. He felt the heavy weight of exhaustion upon him. Then he was startled as the pirogue rocked and Deirdre slid impulsively between his knees and her arms came around his waist. Her hair was disheveled and plucked at by trailing vines, and he felt the soft richness of her body against him and a stirring began, deep inside him.

"We're not lost, are we?" she asked.

"We'll do better in the daylight. Don't be afraid."

"I'm not," she said. "Not when I'm with you."

Insects settled on them in thick swarms, now that the pirogue was motionless. He knew that by morning they might be half maddened by their bites. Backward, there was nothing except darkness and the faint luminescence of secret channels like fingers prodding at the hummocks of soggy land. Pursuit had ended.

He began paddling again to leave the insects behind. A dark mass loomed ahead, blacker than their surroundings. It was an old Indian mound, one of hundreds scattered through the delta country. Tall oaks were limned against the misty sky on the flattened top of the island. Durell grounded the

pirogue on an old shell beach that once might have been
the outermost reach of the delta.

"If there's a spring on top," he said, "we'll stay for the
night."

He helped Deirdre up the embankment. There was fresh
water. They drank quickly of the surprisingly clear, cold
stream that bubbled up in a pool between the gloomy oaks.
All about them in the dark, the life of the swamp was expressed in clicks and small shrieks and hummings and the
occasional deeper grunt of a wild pig.

Deirdre was pale in the dim night. "Can they find us
here?"

"Not likely. And we'll only blunder about in circles if
we go on now."

"Good. Then we're safe."

"For tonight," Durell said.

"Tonight can be a lifetime for us," she said quietly. "I
want to make it so, Sam."

He leaned toward her and folded her in his arms. There
was wild beauty to her that made her look primitive and ele-
mental. Her mouth was open, lips glistening. He held her
tighter and felt her body tremble, pressed tightly against his.
Their kiss was slow and searching and hungry. For just a
moment, then, he thought of Lew Osbourn and Sidonie, but
that was in another place and another time, and he knew that
the girl in his arms was more important to him than anything
else he had ever known.

Desire mounted, shook them both, became a storm that
could not be denied as they came together in the darkness of the swamp that teemed and seethed with noisy life.

Chapter Seventeen . . .

Durell awoke quietly in the chill wet dawn. The world was a vague, misty bowl surrounding the mound on which they had spent the night. Deirdre still slept. She lay with one arm across him, her face turned against his chest. Her breathing was soft and regular. He saw the scratches on her cheek, made by the brush, the smudge of mud on her chin, the stray strands of dark hair across her forehead.

Durell did not move. He let his mind drift backward, remembering the hours of the night. He knew that with Deirdre, as with him, this was not something casual, to be lived and forgotten. But when he looked at her now, she seemed remote and detached from him, strangely aloof, yet a child without defenses or strength. He watched the mist move in gray streamers through the moss hanging from the oak branches above. The sun was up, but it would be an hour before a stray beam could slant through the swamp foliage overhead. He knew how quickly the temperature would soar then, and when he considered where they were and the day that loomed ahead, he was touched by agony for her and what she might suffer.

When he looked at her again, her eyes were open, almost golden in the gray dawn, watching him. She smiled and nestled in the bend of his arm.

"Good morning, darling."

"Hello," he said.

"I love you, darling."

He kissed her. "Hungry?"

"Oh, yes. Ravenous. I'd like—let me see—a mango or a Persian melon, bacon and eggs done just so, lots of *brioches* and coffee, pots and pots of coffee. I think, though, I'll settle for a simple drink of water."

He grinned. "Coming right up."

"Do you have any idea where we are, Sam?"

"Paradise," he said.

She laughed. "Then I'm glad to be here."

"I'm glad, too," he said simply.

"Sure?"

"Never surer."

"Then where is Paradise?" she asked.

He laughed. "Twenty miles from nowhere. Let's go."

The pirogue was safely where he had left it. When they were through at the spring, had washed as best they could, Durell helped her into the narrow boat and shoved away from the mound. It was still cool and damp. Wild hibiscus and bougainvillea made splashes of color against the moving mists around them. He judged direction only by marking the most intense area of light as being in the east, and kept it on his right hand to head north. There was no sign of human life anywhere. They might have been alone in a primeval marshland at the very beginning of time.

When he thought ahead, he realized there could be no definite plan of action to cope with the day. Somehow he had to reach McFee. His only concrete objective was to reach Bayou Peche Rouge, where his grandfather might provide some help.

Deirdre sat with her back to the bow, facing him. Her eyes were somber. "What are you thinking of, Sam?"

"You," he said. "And what may happen to us."

She looked around at the tangled swamp. "I wish we could stay here."

"We can't. We can't hide forever."

"I would like to."

The thought of the *Three Belles* and old Jonathan made him feel better, and he drove the paddle into the water with a stronger stroke.

He continued to use the back channels and lagoons, pushing northward. Once they heard a hunter's shots to the east, but it was impossible to find the right waterway through the maze of drifts, and the shots were not repeated. And although a tenderfoot in the delta country would have been hopelessly lost within the first half hour, traveling in circles or losing himself in the deep muck that could swallow a man with only a trace of bubbles to mark his passage, Durell had no fears. He knew this country and his course was set with confidence. His only concern was for Deirdre's comfort. As the heat of the day reached steamy thickness, he knew she was suffering from thirst and hunger.

He soon fell into a rhythm of paddling that was broken only when Deirdre spelled him briefly. The heat was suffocating, the insects a torment that reached new crescendos with each passing hour. By midmorning Durell knew his face was swollen with bites, and Deirdre sat in limp exhaustion, head bowed, stricken by the heat. Most of his efforts were against the sluggish downriver currents made by the main river channel, somewhere to the left. They passed through enormous cypress groves where the shadows of deep evening still prevailed, and now and then they entered vast muskeg reaches where the wild canes grew ten feet high and he marked the channel only by the bend of the vegetation that conformed with the current. They crossed ponds of blazing beauty, aflame with massed blossoms of hyacinth and wild orchids. The life of the swamp spoke noisily all about them, flickering with movement on every hand.

By ten o'clock the narrow waterway they followed suddenly debouched into a wide channel that was clearly used as a canal. The transition from deep marsh to open water came as a shock as the blazing sunlight hit them without the protective foliage to ward off its sting. The pirogue drifted into midstream. Deirdre lifted her head and looked at Durell and smiled.

"It's all right," he said hoarsely.

"Are we there?"

"It will get better now," he said.

There were no boats in sight, no houses, until they went about half a mile upstream. The canal became choked with weeds and underwater grasses and narrowed where the embankment had washed into the water, undercut by spring floods. Durell knew they could expect no water traffic here. He glimpsed the shack ahead with a grateful surge of relief.

It was only a bayouman's camp, rickety and weathered, ready to collapse into the marshy ground. There was a small landing and, more important, a flat-bottomed rowboat with an old outboard motor. Nobody was in sight. Durell stopped paddling and felt the burn of aching muscles across his back. He saw Deirdre lick her dry, puffed lips. She straightened stiffly and fended off the bow of the pirogue as they came into the landing.

Nobody challenged them. There was only oiled paper over the windows of the shack, and no screens. The door was open. Inside there was a rusted oil stove, an iron cot with a thin straw mattress, a shelf holding canned food over the stove, a kerosene lamp.

There was a thick, rancid smell in the place, like that of an animal's lair.

He searched the place thoroughly. Somebody had slept here the night before, judging from the rumpled cot. Three cane fishing poles leaned against one wall. Durell surveyed the canned food, feeling hunger pangs in him, and as he reached for a can of soup to heat on the kerosene stove, a voice spoke from the doorway over Deirdre's quick gasp.

"Put it down, mister, and git."

Durell turned and saw a gaunt, bony man with an unkempt beard standing beside the girl, who shrank aside. The man wore a gray shirt and gray suspenders and the color of his skin was that of his clothes. He carried a new, shining Remington pump gun.

Durell said easily, "We've been lost in the swamp and haven't eaten since yesterday."

"Git, I said."

"We're hungry and thirsty. We'd like help getting back to town. Maybe you'll give us a lift with your kicker."

The gray man looked at Deirdre and then at Durell and nothing changed in his face. It was a knotty slab of weathered cypress.

"I'm not goin' anywhere today. I got my traps to run."

"Then let me hire your kicker. I'll send it back tonight."

"I tol' you, I got to run traps today."

"Look, I'm not asking help for nothing," Durell said patiently. "I'll pay you. Will ten dollars be enough?"

"I'm busy today."

"Twenty?"

"Git," said the gray man.

Durell said angrily, "How much do you want to help us?"

"I got nothin' to sell you."

"All right," said Durell. "We'll go."

"You got a gun on you, mister. I can see it. Leave it here."

Durell took his gun from his pocket and tossed it to the cot and started through the door. The muzzle of the rifle followed him in a brief arc. As he passed the gray man, Durell jumped and knocked the pump gun aside and hit the bayouman with all his strength. As the man sprawled in the saw grass, Durell picked up the rifle. Deirdre's face was white. She ran into the cabin and retrieved Durell's gun.

"What kind of man is that?" she asked. "You told him we were lost and hungry!"

Durell made no reply. He watched the bayouman hitch himself backward on his rump until he leaned against the shack. Durell took out a twenty-dollar bill from his sweat-soaked wallet and threw it to the ground. "We're borrowing your boat, outboard, and rifle. You can pick them up in Bayou Peche Rouge."

The bayouman simply looked at him with dull hatred.

It was nearly noon when the high stacks of the *Three Belles* loomed above the oaks on shore. Durell slowed the kicker and the boat eased into the lagoon with a diminished surge of power. He held the .30-08 rifle across his knees and watched the channel open up to reveal the ancient hulk of the old side-wheeler.

The *Three Belles* rested in the mud at the upper end of the lagoon, whose waters appeared black and bottomless. She looked the same as always: a forgotten ghost in a forgotten backwater. The network of guy wires between the twin stacks was festooned with moss. Then the upper decks came into view, still white, with huge antique lettering in red curlicues and ornate serifs spelling out her name. Finally the ginger-bread rails, the wide afterdeck, the squat paddle-wheel housings amidships. Her machinery had long since been sold for scrap.

Forty years ago, in a poker game that lasted from Memphis to New Orleans, Jonathan Durell had won the *Three Belles* on a final double-or-nothing turn of the card. In the midst of a champagne celebration later, word came to him that his wife had died in a fire that destroyed his home at Bayou Peche Rouge. Jonathan had ordered everyone ashore except a skeleton crew to work the steamboat, and had run the side-wheeler downriver and into the bayou and full tilt into the mud ashore, where the blackened ruins of his home still smoldered. He had never left the bayou since.

Durell saw nothing to alarm him. Sunlight winked off broken glass in the salon windows and glimmered on brass in the pilot house, where Jonathan had his sleeping quarters. Yet his nerves jumped in him like tight wires that pulled at his bones and his skin.

Deirdre looked at the old steamboat with soft eyes.

"So this is where you were born. I think it's wonderful."

"The old man is wonderful," Durell said.

"Isn't he here now?"

"He must be. He couldn't be far away."

He eased the boat around the low freeboard of the bow and cut off the kicker. The racketing sound of the motor died away across the lagoon, pillowed in the stately oaks and cypress trees. Silence crept in after the echoes. The air was hot and still.

The old man might be asleep. He might have taken a pirogue and gone fishing for his supper. He might be sick. He might be dead.

"Grandpa!" he called.

His words had a strange, muffled quality. The echoes rolled back and forth, back and forth. There was no answer.

"Come on," he said to Deirdre.

He tied up to the stern of the hulk and helped Deirdre to the deck. He did not know what he had expected here, but ever since he had settled on the *Three Belles* as their destination, he had looked forward to its peace and beauty as an oasis of serenity, where time was endless and unchanging. His nerves felt raw. He held the rifle ready as he led the way across the vine-grown deck toward the lacy stairway that lifted up to the once plush cabin deck. From this height they looked out over the clearing where Jonathan's fire-gutted house of forty years ago made a mound of vines and young cypress trees, with here and there a black beam exposed. The twin chimneys stood stark against the hot, murky sky. Anxiety clutched him, honed sharp by the silence. A hundred boyhood memories came back to him. He remembered climbing the giant rusted rocker arms that turned the paddle wheels, exploring the dusty, mysterious staterooms and the vast echoes of the boilers; he remembered fishing off the stern, swimming in the lagoon, climbing the rickety stacks while his grandfather shouted in alarm. . . .

"Sam," Deirdre said. "Is anything wrong?"

"I don't know." He had stopped in the wide corridor that led forward to the pilothouse. "It smells like a trap."

"But who could know about this place?"

He was irritable. "Washington. Weederman. Anybody."

He started walking ahead of the girl. Better get it over with. He went into the wide pilothouse, where the sun shone through old curved glass windows and glinted on the brass fittings of the wheel. Even as he stepped across the threshold, he knew. So he was not surprised.

Swayney was there, and Art Greenwald. And his grandfather.

"Drop the rifle, Sam," Swayney said. "Stand aside from the girl."

Deirdre turned as if to run. Durell caught her arm. "It's all right," he said. "Stand over there. Don't be afraid."

Swayney laughed. Art Greenwald looked embarrassed. Durell said, "Hello, Grandpa."

The white-haired old man in a maritime uniform said gravely, "Better drop the rifle, boy. They've been waiting here since dawn. They mean business. I'm sorry I couldn't warn you off."

"It's all right, Grandpa."

"It isn't all right. I'm ashamed of myself. But there was nothing I could do."

Durell put the rifle down. He felt tired; his bones ached. In a way, he felt relieved. Burritt Swayney looked smug and satisfied. It seemed strange to see him out of his Washington office, away from his desk. His pursy mouth was tight with disapproval as he looked at the girl, but the triumph was there in his codfish eyes, in the way he picked up the pump gun and handed it to Art Greenwald. Art still looked embarrassed, as if all this was painful to him.

Durell shook hands with his grandfather. The old man looked tall and straight and wonderful. "You're in a mess of trouble, boy. It seems you failed to cover your bets."

"I'll be all right."

"Are these gentlemen really from Washington?"

"That's right."

"They think you are a traitor."

"It's a mistake. It will all be straightened out."

"Is this your woman?"

Durell looked at Deirdre and smiled. "Yes," he said.

Her face was white and frightened.

The pilothouse was comfortably furnished. There were several rocking chairs and a day bed and a woven rug on the floor. The old man's books were tiered against one mahogany-planked wall. A desk stood against the huge brass-trimmed wheel. The bayou beyond the windows looked sunny and peaceful. A ship's clock ticked and then rang eight times. It was noon of the third of July.

Swayney's voice was thick with complacent satisfaction. "Sit down, Sam. You've raised enough hell. You can relax now. It's all over. You know it's over, hey? You had us all fooled. Even McFee. He believed in you, when you went to him over my head."

"You son-of-a-bitch," Durell said. "That's all that gripes you."

Swayney smiled; his fat figure rocked easily in his chair. "Let me bring you up to date, hey? We've got Cora Neville. She told us the whole story about Weederman. Seems I was wrong there and the man is still alive. She had a love affair with him and he got her to run a few errands for him over in Germany and she didn't know she was acting for a spy until it was too late. Then he threatened to expose her if she didn't continue to co-operate. So she helped him by making the play for Calvin Padgett. We've got it all down pat in her statement."

"And Weederman?" Durell asked.

"He got away, but he won't get far."

"And Calvin Padgett?"

"We found the boy. Then we went after you. You took feet pretty fast, Sam. You should have listened to my orders when I spoke to you on the telephone. But it didn't matter. We had a tap on Hazel's line, thanks to Art, here. We got that fellow Olsen and he spilled about the whole airfield network. Quite a setup. We did pretty good on cleaning that up, alone. Then we figured where you might land next. You jumped the gun on us and beat us to Jamie's field, but we found your pilot there. They killed him."

Durell winced.

"Once we had you spotted in this territory, it was just a matter of waiting you out. We've crippled Weederman's apparatus. Clobbered it good. You look like you had a hard time last night."

"We spent it in the swamp," Durell said harshly. He didn't like Swayney's satisfaction. He knew there was more coming. Art Greenwald didn't meet his gaze; Art held his gun as if he hated it. His grandfather looked troubled, too, studying

Deirdre. "What else is there? I've got Calvin Padgett's papers. Cyclops must not be launched tomorrow."

"Cyclops will be launched," Swayney said quietly. "She goes up at four o'clock in the afternoon."

"Just as it is?"

"There's nothing wrong with the hardware."

"Is that McFee's word?"

"When I told McFee about your girl, he gave me the white slip on handling you, Sam. You've been played right over the barrel." Swayney stood up; his manner changed. His voice was hostile and implacable. "I hate a man who makes a fool of himself like you've done, Sam. Maybe you aren't selling us out, or maybe you just don't know what kind of a ride this babe has given you. Have you still got Padgett's papers?"

"Yes, I have them," Durell said.

Swayney looked at the girl. "I'm surprised you didn't get them off him yet. You must have felt pretty sure of Sam, hey?"

"What are you talking about?" Durell asked.

Swayney hooked a fat hip on a corner of the desk. "Did Deirdre Padgett tell you about her boy friend who was killed in Korea?"

"Yes, she mentioned it."

"Once over lightly, hey? Did she say she was married to him?"

Durell felt the shock. "No. Is that true, Deirdre?"

She would not look at him.

Swayney said, "Did she tell you how this husband of hers, Robert Keitch, happened to get himself dead over there?"

"Deirdre?" Durell said.

She would not look at him.

"He was a prisoner of war," Swayney said, "along with a lot of other guys who were caught short over there when the Chinese put their fat fingers in the Korean pie. But Keitch was different. This little lady had a husband who knew how to take good care of himself. He did good in prison, didn't he, baby? So good he was known as a pro-Red and he elected to stay over there. But at the last minute one of the boys got him. One of the boys who'd been strung up by the thumbs in a barrel of ice water because Keitch played footsie with the guards and told them about a planned prison break. So our own boys took care of Keitch. That's the guy she loved and married."

"I don't believe it," Durell whispered.

"Ask her."

"Deirdre?"

She would not look at him.

"Tell him," Swayney said. He slid off the desk, crossed the room, stood in front of the girl. Her face was white. "Tell him how you and your subversive rat of a brother made a deal with Weederman to sell the plans for Cyclops, and how your brother held out for a bigger bonus and crossed Weederman. That's why they leaned on you so hard, isn't it? And that's why you played for Sam the way you did. They killed your brother, but you still held out for the price, hey? I can't figure people like you. I can't see it. But there you stand. Go ahead and tell Sam. Tell him the truth."

She said nothing.

Chapter Eighteen . . .

Durell said stiffly, "Are we under arrest?"

"Let's say you're in custody," Swayney said.

"Do you go along with that, Art?"

Greenwald looked embarrassed. "I'm sorry, Sam. Swayney is the boss."

"I'm touched," Swayney said. "Art, get some cuffs on the girl. She got away once, she'll try it again, hey?"

"I'm sorry," Greenwald said again.

He stood up, a young man with curly black hair and a troubled face. Deirdre stood stiffly, motionless. Sunlight glinted on the cuffs Greenwald produced. It was hot in the pilothouse. In that moment, Durell's mind probed for an elusive element in the pattern around him, something disturbing, not quite within reach. He heard the calls and songs of the birds in the trees; he heard the splash of a fish in the lagoon. There was nothing else.

"Wait a moment," he said. "Be reasonable. We're tired and we're hungry. Can't we have something to eat?"

Jonathan said gently, "I have some court bouillon and redfish in the galley, boy. If these gentlemen will let me get it . . ."

Swayney hesitated. "All right. Sit down, Art. You, too, Miss Padgett."

Deirdre sat down stiffly. Her face was a blank mask. Durell looked at his grandfather and felt overcome by a deep wave of affection and love for the old man. Jonathan went out.

"There's a car coming for us from New Orleans," Swayney said. He looked at his watch. "We'll be moving out in half an hour."

"The sooner, the better," Durell said. "I want to see Dickinson McFee."

"Sorry. We're holding you both at the FBI offices in New Orleans."

"I want to go to Washington. Burritt, it's important!"

"You will stay where I put you. Both you and your girl friend."

"At least, will you let me talk to McFee on the phone?"

"No. What do you take me for, Sam? I know what you're thinking," Swayney said angrily. "But on the one hand, I've got the word from all the Las Tiengas people that everything has been checked and double-checked. You can't just throw out a schedule and firing time that hundreds of people have planned on for over two years! And what have I got to balance all that weight? Calvin Padgett, a traitor, a psychotic, soft-minded subversive. And his sister, who's made a monkey out of you. She didn't deny a word I said, did she? You ought to smarten up, Sam, and admit that you're wrong."

Durell said nothing. He heard the birds outside, the splash of fish in the lagoon. His mind reached forward into tomorrow. He saw the faltering missile in flight, he saw the flame and smoke of its arching trajectory. He saw it reach for the vast ocean of space and then respond to the mortal flaw in the myriad of bright relays and tubes and transistors that composed its brain. It plummeted back to the earth that had given it birth.

Explosion . . . desolation . . . death . . .

He could not let it happen.

No matter what he had to do. And no matter about Deirdre.

Jonathan was taking a long time getting the soup from the galley. Much too long. The galley was only down on the lower deck, a few steps from the wide staircase. . . . Durell's mind suddenly tensed with alarm, with sudden relief, with gratitude.

His grandfather stood in the doorway of the pilothouse, holding a twelve-gauge over-and-under shotgun casually, easily, intimately. It was pointed at Swayney.

The old man said, "I regret the necessity of this, gentlemen. I am a loyal citizen, I assure you. But so is my grandson. Kindly drop your weapons, sirs."

Swayney turned purple. Art Greenwald looked as if he wanted to smile and then the shotgun twitched just a little in his direction and he dropped his gun. Swayney said something incoherent.

"Why, you stupid, blundering, senile old man—"

"I take that unkindly, sir," said Jonathan. "Samuel, if you wish to go now, you may go."

Durell stood up. He retrieved the pump gun. He looked at the girl. "Deirdre?"

"Take me with you," she whispered. It was the first time she had spoken in several long minutes. "Please, Sam."

"Of course," he said.

The old man said, "I'll meet you at the twins. Where I cut you that fishpole. You remember, Samuel?"

"I remember." Durell looked at Swayney and Art Greenwald. "Can you hold them, Grandpa?"

"I can do anything," the old man said gravely. "Within reason, of course."

Durell touched Deirdre's arm and they went out through a side door. Swayney shouted something vituperative after him, but he paid no attention. The side door led to the open topmost deck, between the huge rusted rocker arms that had once helped to power the old side-wheeler. The sun was hot, blazing. The black water of the lagoon seemed to suck up all the light when Durell looked down over the side of the old vessel. There was no sound from behind them. He drew a deep breath, then led the girl quickly down the staircase to the afterdeck and then along the rickety gangplank to the shore. He kept the bulk of the old side-wheeler between himself and the pilothouse windows so that Swayney would not be able to determine their direction.

Deirdre stumbled and he held her arm for a moment and helped her upright. She said nothing more. Perspiration glistened on her pale face. Beyond the ruins of the gutted house ashore, a narrow trail led them into the dense shadows of the swamp. Durell paused and listened. There was still no sound from the hulk. He said a prayer for his grandfather and plunged on. The trail twisted and lifted and fell through the brush and swamp. When they had gone on for five minutes, a little glade opened before them, a grassy clearing on the bank of a shallow pool sheltered by a curiously twisted double oak and massive, drooping willows. Durell halted. Deirdre breathed with difficulty beside him.

"We'll wait here for him."

"Suppose he doesn't come?"

"He'll be here."

"What can an old man do against people like Swayney?"

"Don't underestimate him," Durell said. "He'll show up."

She sank down on the grass and buried her face in her hands. Durell stood beside her. The jacket of her rust-red suit was torn and stained by their night in the swamp. He saw the coppery glint of her hair, and remembered the soft and flesh-warm miracle of her body as she had been last night. Confusion tore at him.

"Deirdre," he said. "Deirdre, why didn't you deny the things Swayney said about you?"

"I couldn't."

"Are they true?"

"What do you think?"

"I'm simply asking."

"Yes," she said. "You're asking."

"What's the matter?"

"You believed Swayney completely, at once."

"Were you really married to Robert Keitch?"

"Yes, I was."

"Was he the man Swayney described?"

"Yes."

"Why didn't you tell me about it?"

"It would have made a difference."

"What makes you think so?"

She looked up at him. "It makes a difference now, doesn't it?"

"I don't know," he said bluntly.

"Well, that's why I didn't tell you."

There seemed to be nothing more to be said between them. The little glade was quiet except for the humming of the insects. Durell felt tired. He sat down and plucked a blade of grass and chewed on it. An eternity ago, a lifetime away, in another world, he had come here with his grandfather and old Jonathan had cut willow poles from those huge old willows and taught him to fish in the little pond before him. It was in another reality, not this one. He shook with exhaustion. He felt hunger and thirst. He wondered if it was worth while to go on. The last of his bridges had been burned behind him now.

Suddenly he hated himself and everything he had done.

The old man arrived fifteen minutes later. He looked

calm and unhurried. He carried the shotgun in one hand, a bag of sandwiches and bottles of beer in the other. His quiet old eyes regarded the stiff figure of the girl, then swung to Durell.

"You are betting everything on one throw of the dice, Samuel. That is not the way I taught you to gamble."

"I can't help it, Grandpa. This is the way it has to be. I'm only sorry I got you involved in this."

"I'm enjoying it," the old man said.

"But you won't dare go back to the *Three Belles* now."

"After a time, a man can find himself living too long with souvenirs and memories that have no life in them. It isn't living. You talk to your woman yet?"

"Yes," Durell said.

The old man said, "I can see you didn't say the right things. She looks like a fine girl to me." He spoke as if Deirdre were not right beside him. "You're a fool about some things, Samuel."

"What did you do with Swayney and Greenwald?"

"They're locked up in the old engine room. They can get out easily enough, but it will take them a bit of time before they find the way. No harm is done."

"I've got to get to Washington, Grandpa."

"I've been thinking about that. It won't be hard. Howie Gregory runs an air-freight service for the Bayou Peche Rouge Fishery. He flies quick, refrigerated planes so that the Yankees can enjoy our fine Gulf shrimp. Six hours to New York. Sometimes less. The airplanes are not fancy, but there won't be any questions asked if I tell Howie to take you and the girl."

"When does he fly, and from where?"

"Every afternoon. The field is about four miles from here, on the bayou landing at Peche Rouge. There won't be any trouble about it."

"What will you do?"

The old man smiled. "I'm going to New Orleans and start building up a fresh set of souvenirs for me to think about."

"Let's go," Durell said. Then: "Deirdre?"

She had held herself aloof and apart from the conversation. Now she looked at Durell with cool challenge in her gray eyes. "Are you sure you trust me?"

"I trust you," he said.

The DC-3 was cold, their accommodations crude bucket seats in a tiny compartment wedged between the pilot's cabin and the sealed bulkheads of the refrigeration units. The pilot had nodded to them and then had not spoken afterward. The airfield adjoining the shrimp canneries and the levee wharves had been crowded and no one paid any attention to them. Now the sun was low in the west behind them as they flew over Mississippi and Alabama.

Durell could not endure Deirdre's silence.

"What is it?" he asked.

"Nothing."

"Why have you changed?"

"I haven't changed. I'm the same as I ever was."

"No. It's like when you first met me. Hating me. Fighting me all the way."

"I don't hate you."

"Do you regret anything?"

"Only the look on your face when Swayney told you about me."

Atlanta was a field of lights twinkling against the purple fold of the land at evening. The air was bumpy, and now and then they ran through spattering rain, remnant of the weather front that had forced them south last night. Then Atlanta was gone, lost behind them as they flew into the darkening night.

Durell slept. He dreamed. The bright missile lit up the sky, struggling toward free space and failing, then falling, fusing. Explosion! Where? In empty fields, on desolate mountains? Or on crowded cities, helpless families, fragile homes? An ugly mushroom lifted to the cloud on a flame-shot stalk, bringing destruction, desolation, death.

Durell twisted and fought in his sleep. He cried out, and Deirdre's hands were on his face and her voice whispered anxiously, "Sam? Sam!"

He awoke. He was cold. He sweated and shivered.

"You were dreaming," she said. "It must have been horrible."

"It will be," he said.

"You can stop it," she said. "Can't you?"

"I'm alone."

"That's not true," she said. "I'm with you."

"And I need you."

"I'll do anything."

He said it. "I love you."

Love and hate, pain and joy. His thoughts blurred and became a misty mirror that reflected lights below, darkness above, the heavy pulsing of the engines. He felt as if he had been flying forever. His eyes ached, his nerves plucked at his bones, his fingertips screamed.

She kissed him. "Sleep, Sam. You've got to rest."

"After I see McFee. After he listens to me."

She said, "There's something else I want to tell you about Robert Keitch."

He felt anger. "I don't want to hear it."

"But I *must* talk about him. Please!"

He was silent.

"We were in love," she said quietly. "We thought that's what it was. He was kind and gentle. Too kind; too gentle. He was soft. He was a coward. What he needed was a woman who would mother him. I couldn't do it. When he was drafted into the Army, we were already far apart. Living in the same house, sharing the same bedroom, but as far apart as if the world stood between us. Maybe it did. Perhaps I was wrong to reject him, to try to force him to be a man. I was married to him, I tried to help him. But I couldn't. It was something in him—or something that wasn't in him—something basic, that I couldn't help him with. When he went to Korea, we both knew it was all over. And when I heard about him and the things he did when he was a prisoner, I felt as if it was my fault, all my fault."

"No," Durell said. "How could it be?"

She was crying silently. "I should have been able to help him."

"Some men can't be helped. They don't want it."

"I could have tried harder to understand why he resisted everything so much. Why he always looked for easy things, the easy way."

"Deirdre, stop this."

"I just want you to know about it. I don't want you always to remember the way Swayney told you about Robert. I keep hearing the sound of Swayney's voice the way he told you. It haunts me. It will kill me."

There was rain against the plane windows, rain that filled the dark, windy sky. There was the earth and this was the sky and up above was that ultimate dark sea, that infinite space, that ineffable mystery that called man toward it though

his steps tottered and faltered. Was it right to take that
first step with a knife in one's hand, poised at the throat of
all mankind? Humanity carried in it the seeds of its own
destruction, never more pressing or potent than in these
warped and troubled days. Was it right to take that first
step, to create a new star, a stage for further steps that
would surpass it by progressing into the awesome sea of
space? And would it bring peace? He did not think so.
Whether this nation or that nation seemed to control the
ultimate weapon was always an illusion that crumbled in
the inexorable tide of history.

What is the matter with me? Durell cried silently.

He searched in the dark emptiness beyond the plane window, but he saw no answer out there. Maybe Cyclops would
give the world a breathing spell, a time in which to pause
and consider and view the brink of destruction where man
had stumbled and threatened to fall. If only for that, he
thought, it would be enough. If it gained time . . .

He looked at Deirdre for the answer.

He saw in her face no questions of tormenting universal
importance. He saw in her face only her concern for him,
her love for him, naked and beautiful and unashamed, plead-
ing with him for his understanding.

It's enough, he thought, and in the end this is what it
comes down to, to have someone, to be complete, to give
and to share and to feel the enveloping warmth of another
human being's love.

Far below on the looming curve of the earth, he saw
twinkling lights and a strange complex of radiance, and he
saw it was a small town, and a carnival of some kind, guess-
ing this by the tiny circlet of light that could only be a Ferris
wheel, the undulating lights of a roller coaster. As he
watched, lights bloomed below the plane, a burst of reds
and greens and blues and yellows. Rockets. Durell looked
at his watch.

It was midnight. It was the Fourth of July.

Chapter Nineteen . . .

The Glorious Fourth.

A day for political oratory, a brave display of flags, picnics, fireworks, a drive in the country, sleeping, eating, swimming, making love under a free sky.

It was two o'clock in the morning when Durell got off the bus from the airport with Deirdre. He took a cab to the neighborhood of his apartment, got out a block away, and walked with the girl through the warm summer night, through the dark pools of shadow under the poplar and sycamore trees. Nobody was watching his apartment house. It seemed a long time since he was here last. The circle was completed, waiting for him to forge the final link here in Washington, where it had begun.

He had considered contacting Sidonie Osbourn and sending Deirdre to her in the Alexandria house, but Deirdre would not go. He checked front and rear entrances to his apartment building. Nobody. They went inside. Nothing was changed. His rooms were as he had left them.

The apartment looked less drab with Deirdre moving about in the rooms. She went into the bath and after a few moments he heard the hiss of the shower. He rubbed a hand over his jaw, felt the bristles of his beard; he needed a shave and clean-up badly. He went to the telephone and dialed Hazel Getcher's number.

There were two rings, a click. "Yes?"

"Hazel," he said.

"Hang up." She recognized his voice. "Hang up, please."

"I know you're tapped, Hazel. It's all right. Where is the boss? Is he back from New York yet?"

"Yes, he's back."

"What's the matter?"

"He's not for you any more. He's been talked to. He's been persuaded. Don't go there."

"I've got to go there. At his home?"

"Please!"

"Take care," Durell said. He hung up. The shower had stopped. He built two drinks in his kitchen and brought them back to the living room and Deirdre came out of the bath, wearing his old robe. She looked smaller in her bare feet and the oversized garment; her face was scrubbed and glowing. She looked wonderful. "Get dressed," he said. "We've got to move out of here."

Alarm crawled in her eyes and disappointment shadowed her mouth. She bit her lip. "So soon? Oh, Sam. . . ."

"Let's go," he said.

He shaved while she dressed in the rust-red suit again. She used his comb and brushes to straighten her long hair. She smiled ruefully. "I look awful, Sam. I haven't had a change of clothes or any make-up for days. How can you love me?"

"It's easy," he said, smiling. "Hurry."

The streets were warm and soft with the summer night. He got his car from the garage without difficulty and he began to feel optimistic and was no longer tired. He felt as if he were about to make a fresh start, and he whistled softly as he drove, and then he heard the sound of his whistling and it surprised him. His feeling of optimism grew. He knew Dickinson McFee would believe him. He had Calvin Padgett's papers in his pocket. As a last resort, he decided, he would call the news syndicates and give them enough of the story so that a furor would be raised in the press and on the radio—enough pressure to postpone the launching of Cyclops.

Deirdre was shivering. He could feel it as she sat close beside him in the car.

"Are you afraid?" he asked.

"Yes. For you. For both of us. For the whole world. I've never been so afraid."

Dickinson McFee lived in a narrow limestone house on Connecticut Avenue. It was set back from the street behind a high iron fence, partially hidden from the wide avenue by Japanese maples and two huge sycamores. Durell drove slowly by and saw that the sidewalks were deserted and saw a light shining in a window on the second floor. The line of parked cars stretched from one corner to the next. The street was asleep. There was no sign of special activity except for the lighted window. He went around the block again, then turned into a broad, brick-paved alley that bisected the block and ran behind the row of residences that included McFee's. More cars were parked here, but there was room for Durell's coupé near the far exit, and he parked there.

"Stay in the car," he told Deirdre. "If anything goes wrong, get away from here fast."

"I'd rather go in with you."

He shook his head. "It will be better if I see McFee alone. It will only complicate things if you're there, too."

She was worried. "Are you taking your gun with you?"

He hadn't thought about it. He had grown accustomed to its weight in his inside pocket. "Why not?"

"I wish you'd leave it here with me. I'd feel better about it. You're in enough trouble with your people as it is."

He put the gun on the leather seat. "You're probably right."

As he walked down the brick-paved alley, some of his optimism waned. The tall ailanthus trees in the back yards behind wooden fences cast motionless pools of deep shadow. From one of the houses came a chatter of French and a drone of music. The back of General McFee's house was sheltered by a tall board fence with a gate in it, and beyond the gate was a small lawn and a flagstone patio. Durell had been here to dinner on several occasions, and he knew that because of the difficulty of parking on the street, this back entrance was used more often than the formal front entry. He tried the gate. It was not locked, and he stepped quietly into the dark back garden. From inside the house came the shrill ringing of a telephone.

There was a light in the kitchen, a heavy scent of blossoms in the air. Durell crossed the back yard quickly, then squeezed through the screened kitchen doorway. A colored man in a white starched jacket paused as he reached inside a pantry shelf. Durell knew him—Jeffry had been with Dickinson McFee for years—and he saw that Jeffry knew him, too. All about him. The man's eyes widened and he started to speak, but Durell interrupted him.

"You're up late, Jeffry. Is the General at home? I've come to see him."

The butler looked frightened. "I reckon the General wants to see you, too, sir, Mr. Durell. I—I'll buzz him."

Durell moved quickly and pulled Jeffry's hand from the wall telephone. He said, "Don't do that." He spoke quietly. "You don't have to be afraid of me."

Jeffry spoke haltingly. "I don't understand. They—they're lookin' for you all over creation, Mr. Durell."

Durell's smile was stiff in the face of Jeffry's obvious fear. "Let's go find the General."

He followed hard on Jeffry's heels. Without warning, his heart began to hammer heavily, and for no reason at all he suddenly felt he had made a fatal mistake. But it was too late to turn back. Jeffry went down a long dim hallway and started up a graceful staircase.

"Wait a moment," Durell said. "Is anyone else in the house besides you and the General?"

"No, sir."

"You're sure?"

"Yes, sir."

At the head of the stairs, Jeffry pointed to a door at the end of the hall. "General McFee is in his study. Will that be all?"

Durell smiled. "Come with me."

"I have work to do, sir."

"You know what I mean," Durell said. "I wouldn't like to think you might call the police while I was with the General. Go ahead, Jeffry. And when we get inside, just sit down in a chair where I can see you. And don't try to leave. Do you understand?"

"Yes, sir."

From inside the room came the sound of McFee's voice, apparently on the telephone that Durell had heard ringing when he was out in the back yard. Jeffry knocked and Durell pushed him inside and quickly closed the door.

Dickinson McFee looked up with the telephone poised in his hand. His eyes were shocked.

"Put it down," Durell said. "Quick."

McFee breathed out. "I'll be triple damned."

"I mean it, General. Now."

McFee did not move. His eyes were bright and penetrating, pale and cool, intelligent and remote. His mouth twitched. He covered the telephone mouthpiece with his hand before he spoke.

"Are you armed, Sam?"

"Yes," Durell said, and he wished he hadn't yielded to

Deirdre's sudden request that he give up his gun before coming in here. "Say good-by and hang up, whoever it is."

"I'm talking to General Aiken. He's here from Las Tiengas."

"Hang up," Durell insisted.

McFee took his hand from the mouthpiece and spoke calmly. "I'll call back. Something important has just come up." He put the telephone down with slow care. His small physique seemed to expand, filling the room with his personality. He looked at the colored man. "You can go, Jeffry."

"I want him where I can see him," Durell said.

"Then sit down, Jeffry. You're not afraid of Sam, are you? Sit down and try not to hear too much."

Durell leaned back against the door. His mouth felt dry. He looked at McFee and wished he had been greeted in almost any other manner than this cool objectivity.

"General," he said, "I've come a long way. I'm tired and I'm confused and you're the only man I can count on to listen. You sent me out there, you told me to trust nobody. I tried to get you on the phone, but it was always impossible. So I'm here. It wasn't easy to get here. But I've had no choice. All I want is for you to listen to me."

"I'm listening," McFee said.

"And believe me."

"That depends."

For a moment Durell felt defeated, with no will to go on. He stared blankly at McFee and saw beyond even this man the mindless efficiency of government bureaus, the maze of routine that formed a dark labyrinth in which a simple truth could be hopelessly lost. It was very quiet in the house. He thought of Deirdre, sitting alone in the car outside. A man had to trust his hunches. He forced his mind back to McFee, seated at the desk.

"General," he said quietly, "would I have come here if I had done anything wrong? Would I have come to you if I were guilty of treason, as Swayney says I am?"

"I admit I am surprised. You've cut a wide swath, Sam."

"It was necessary. Nobody would listen. I'm not saying that Aiken or Larabee or Swayney meant wrong, or tried to suppress me because of treasonous motives. But your own instructions forced me to do what I did." Durell took out the sheaf of calculations he had carried so far. McFee didn't touch them when Durell tossed them to the desk. "Calvin

Padgett was not permitted the use of an electronic computer to check these equations. They'll show a need to delay the Cyclops launching. That's all he wanted. And I don't ask for anything more than having these figures checked. If they're wrong, then I've been wrong. But if they're right, then you'll know what must be done about Cyclops. You can't afford not to check them."

McFee said, "I've talked to Swayney, General Aiken, and Larabee. And I've been talked *at* by the Pentagon, Joint Chiefs, and the White House. There can be no delay in getting Cyclops off the ground and into patrol orbit."

"But Cyclops will not orbit. It won't break away from earth's gravity pull. It will come down——"

"Wait." McFee waved a slim hand. "Every priority has been given to launching Cyclops as soon as possible. Now General Aiken and Larabee brought me the medical records on Calvin Padgett, and Swayney brought in the dossiers on Padgett's sister and her husband. Swayney says the girl simply took you for a sweet ride."

Durell felt sudden anger. "She never asked me for anything. There's nothing wrong about her *or* Calvin Padgett. I know it. I feel it. Why won't you listen? Are you afraid for your own skin, General? Have the bureaucrats paralyzed you, too?"

"Shut up," McFee said tightly.

"Why? Isn't it true that you're afraid to risk your own judgment and order Cyclops grounded? Just check these figures of Cal Padgett's. Is that asking too much? All I request is that you keep an open mind."

McFee stood up, both hands on the desk, near the sheaf of paper Durell had tossed there. His eyes were cold and inimical. Jeffry moved in his chair and the leather creaked. Abruptly the telephone began to ring again. McFee did not look at it. The sound was shrill and strident, tearing at Durell's nerves.

Durell drew a deep breath when the ringing stopped.

"All I came here for was to get some help on this. I came to deliver these equations on your desk, to get somebody to look at them and do what has to be done. I'm not sure who the traitor is. I think it's John Padgett, but I can't prove anything. Yet somebody gimmicked the relays in Cyclops' brain so it will run amok. It won't orbit. It will go up in an arc and come down somewhere on the continental United States and its warhead will spray bombs over a wide area. It can destroy us all. Somebody has to do something about it. If you won't help, I don't know what else to do, because time is running out and in a few hours somebody will push a button and it will happen."

McFee said quietly, "You're under arrest, Sam. Give me your gun."

"No."

The telephone rang again. It rang four times and was silent. Durell saw that McFee did not believe him. He saw it was hopeless. There was nothing he could do.

"Your gun, Sam," McFee said sharply.

Durell said flatly, "I don't have one."

McFee looked surprised. Then he reached in his desk and took out a small revolver and pointed it at Durell. Jeffry made a small sound and sat tightly in his leather chair.

"I'm sorry to do this, Sam," McFee said. "But I can't take any chances. All you have is a hunch, against all the evidence that weighs against you. Come over to the desk. Put your hands flat."

He obeyed. The papers he had put on the desk had been brushed aside. McFee circled him and went over his pockets quickly and deftly. Then Durell's mind suddenly jolted free of his paralysis as he considered the papers before him. McFee had not looked at them. In a world turned upside down, where right was wrong and friends were enemies, he knew what he had to do.

Suddenly he spun on his heel, dropped one shoulder, and slashed at McFee's gun. The edge of his hand struck McFee's wrist and the gun clattered on the floor. McFee yelled and Durell hit him hard and McFee went backward, arms wide, fingers splayed. Durell kicked the gun under the desk. He saw Jeffry lunge up from the chair and he hit Jeffry and the man went down, screaming in a thin, high voice. McFee was standing still, eyes glazed. Durell rubbed his right hand. There was blood on his knuckles.

Jeffry kept on screaming. Durell yanked open the door and plunged into the hall. His legs trembled. He felt sick. For a moment he dragged in deep, retching breaths of air. He couldn't move. From inside the room came the sound of Jeffry clawing under the desk for the gun and still screaming for help. He stumbled on the first stair riser and fell halfway down to the lower floor before he caught himself. His trouser leg was torn and flapping. He stared at it, then went all the way down and trotted through the house to the kitchen. Nobody got in his way. It was only as he crossed the back yard that he remembered Padgett's papers left on McFee's desk. It was too late to go back now. He ran across the yard and opened the gate in the high fence and plunged into the alley, running for Deirdre and his car.

The car was where he had left it. But Deirdre wasn't in it. She was gone.

Chapter Twenty . . .

Durell stared at the empty car and looked up and down the dark driveway and then ran to the exit and looked both ways up and down the street. She was not in sight. He stood as if paralyzed. Even from here he could hear Jeffry's screeching. A man came out of one of the back yards, dressed in pajamas, and stood indecisively in his gateway. He glanced at Durell and trotted back inside. Durell felt as if he could not move without Deirdre. He could not leave without her. He felt desperately alone.

But she was gone. And in the distance was the sound of a siren. The siren made him think of the police, and his mind began to work again. He returned to his car and got in and drove out of the alley. The tires screeched as he turned into the street. He went once around the dark block, hoping for a glimpse of Deirdre. When he returned to the alley entrance, he saw a small crowd gathered at the back of Dickinson McFee's house. He gave up looking for her then and drove away.

Afterward, he was not sure where he went or what roads he took. McFee had failed him; and Deirdre, whom he had trusted, who had convinced him that he ought to undertake the mission when Calvin was killed, was gone. He did not know which blow was worse. He did not try to avoid the police especially; he did not think too much about them. His mind turned and twisted, alternating between the two poles of his problem. He could not understand why Deirdre had left the car. Something must have happened, something had caught her attention. He could not accept the possibility that Swayney was right and she had deserted him. He had gambled on her, on his instinct. If he was wrong, his whole life was wrong. Panic touched him and swelled violently while his mind jumped this way and that, and then the panic subsided and left only a deep hopelessness.

He did not consider the danger to himself when he found himself following the highway to the Chesapeake shore and the Padgett house. A dim hope flickered that somehow Deirdre might have gone there.

The big, empty house on the shore at Prince John was quiet, dreaming under the summer moonlight. It was past three in the morning. Everything was dark. He knew the main house was an empty, abandoned shell. He parked in front of the gate cottage and sat for a moment with his forehead against the cool wheel, then got out and walked around the house, trying the doors. Everything was locked. She was not here.

The Chesapeake glimmered with silver under the light of the moon. He turned and tramped through the weeds toward the main house, a hundred yards away. Crickets sang in the wild grass. There was a warm, steady breeze from over the water. The rose bricks of the old Padgett house looked dark in the silvery light. A shutter banged uneasily. A screen door flapped. He swerved toward the arched opening of what had once been a carriage shed.

A dark sedan was parked here in the darkness. Metal creaked as it cooled. He felt the hood. It was warm.

Durell's head came up sharply. He listened, but there was no sound from the deserted house. Then he turned and crossed the area of waist-high brush that had been a back lawn and tried the kitchen door. It was not locked.

He let the screen door slam behind him. Moonlight lay black on the red Belgian tiles of the floor.

"Deirdre?"

The house was silent.

In the dim light he saw a half-empty bottle of bourbon and a tumbler, partially full, on the kitchen table. A piece of melting ice cube still floated in it. The silence was absolute except for the shrill singing of the crickets outside.

"Deirdre!" he called again.

No answer. A trap? Who could be here? Nobody. Somebody. Close at hand. He quit the kitchen and walked boldly down a wide center corridor to the front of the house. The front door stood open and he could see the Chesapeake shining in the moonlight. A warm wind whined through the empty, dusty house. There was a smell of mildew and decay in the bare walls, the emptily echoing rooms. He looked into a long chamber at his right and saw the dark outlines of a huge brick fireplace and started to turn away, then halted and stood as he was, unable to go farther.

The moonlight showed him a man seated in a dusty, rotting wing chair beside the fireplace, facing him as he stood in the doorway.

Gustav Weederman, alias George West, manager of the Salamander.

Dead.

He told himself it was some mistake. Weederman could not be here. But it was no mistake. Durell walked into the room and halted and saw that Weederman had been shot in the back of the head. The man's hard, handsome face was half blown away. Durell shivered suddenly as if a cold wind had touched him. Weederman's flesh was still warm. The bullet wound in the back of his head was small, but the internal pressure of the slug's impact on the brain had bulged Weederman's eyes grotesquely.

Durell was not startled when he heard a scraping footfall behind him from the hallway entrance. He turned and looked at the man who stood smiling in the moonlight.

"Hello, Mr. Durell."

It was John Padgett. He stood tall and gaunt, leaning heavily on his knobby cane, his predatory head thrust forward a little, bony shoulders hunched, his right hand in his pocket. He might have been standing like that, about to lecture a class in the technology of astrophysics. Or he might have been ready to offer Durell a drink. He looked at ease. He looked deadly.

"Professor Padgett," Durell said.

"Are you surprised, sir?"

"Not really."

"Do you know who that man is?" The heavy stick gestured toward Weederman, dead in his chair.

"I know something about him. He killed your brother."

Padgett smiled, but the smile was different now. "Yes, he did. Life has a way of leveling us all, has it not? Even a man as strong as you, Mr. Durell. As you can see. I am sorry I cannot ask you to be seated. This house is only the ghost of the place it once was. Once it was happy, filled with joy and pleasant people. And this, too, has been leveled."

"Did you kill Weederman?"

"Let us not be foolish."

"You killed him," Durell said. His voice lifted. "You're the one who was double-crossing him. You're the one who gimmicked the brain for Cyclops, who framed Calvin into a strait jacket. In a way, you killed your own brother."

The smile again. The hunched shoulders. The darkly brooding eyes. A sense of physical impairment hiding tremendous power.

"The score has been evened," Padgett said.

"By killing Weederman?"

John Padgett leaned on his cane. "I will not be charged with this matter. Even if I were, it would be considered a patriotic duty to destroy that man. But you, Mr. Durell, are more resourceful than Larabee gave you credit for. No one expected you to come this far. You have traveled a long way. And, of course, you must know that this is the end of the road."

"Not quite," Durell said. "Are you alone here?"

"I have help." Padgett smiled. "Where is my sister?"

"I don't know."

"Deirdre came East with you, did she not?"

"To hell with you," Durell said.

The gaunt, beaked face hardened. "Mr. Durell, there is not much time. I must find Deirdre. And you will tell me where she is."

"No."

Padgett turned slightly. "Franz!"

Franz came into the room, hulking, enormous, his shaved head gleaming in the moonlight that shone through the tall dusty windows. Durell looked at the giant and felt a trembling of hatred go through him. He took a step foward, saw the gun in Franz's hand, and halted.

"Mr. Durell will come with us," Padgett told Franz.

"No," Durell said. But even in his ears, his voice lacked conviction. He had no gun. He was trapped. This was the end of it all. Yet when he looked at the dead man, Weederman, he knew there were some questions still unanswered. And he wanted the answers. He saw that if he fought back now, Franz would kill him. Franz would think no more about it than he would of swatting a fly.

Franz gestured with the gun and Durell walked out of the bare room ahead of them. The wind hissed in the tall weeds of the yard. John Padgett moved along with a clumsy, hitching gait, having trouble even with his heavy cane. They went to the carriage shed and Durell was motioned into the front seat of the car. John Padgett drove. Franz sat in the back with the muzzle of his gun against Durell's neck.

It was only a mile along the dirt lane to the little fishing village of Prince John. Nobody spoke. The gray-shingled houses looked silvery in the moonlight. There were a few darkened stores, a yellow blinker flashing silently at the intersection, a wharf with oyster boats tied up in a row. There were no lights anywhere. There was no other traffic.

Padgett's knobby stick leaned against the front seat between them. Durell drew a deep breath. He kept his hands in his lap. They were following the bay shore, going north on a rough and bumpy dirt road.

Durell said, "Franz, I thought you worked for Weederman."

Franz laughed softly. "So I did."

"And for the cause."

"I worked for the money. It was Weederman who had a cause."

"So you don't care that he's dead?"

"I will not lose sleep over him," Franz rumbled.

"So you don't care that John killed him?"

"Why should I?"

"Maybe the professor will kill you, too."

Franz laughed again. "You talk too much."

"If John doesn't kill you, I will. Do you know that?"

Franz said, "Mister, you are now a dead man."

They went another mile in silence.

Then Durell said, "Professor, do you plan to hold me until Cyclops is launched, at four o'clock this afternoon?"

"Yes."

"Then you think your sabotage effort will succeed?"

"When I am sure of my sister. And when I get Calvin's papers."

Durell said, "You will never see either of them again."

They were passing through another small town. The streets were dark and empty. But there were people nearby—asleep, perhaps, but they could be wakened. Durell put his hand on Padgett's cane and lifted it suddenly, smashing at the man's hands on the wheel; at the same time he reached for the door handle and pushed it down and threw his body to the right.

The door started to open and Padgett lost control of the
car as he involuntarily jerked his crushed hand from the
wheel. Franz yelled. The door was only partly open; the latch
had caught. The car left the road and bounced up on the
sidewalk. Franz leaned over Durell and grabbed at the wheel.
Durell tried to twist his gun away. It was like trying to
twist a bar of steel. He threw himself at the balky door
and felt it open and the car careened back onto the street
again and he felt himself falling out. Something caught his
coat and from the corner of his eye he saw Franz looming
enormously over him from the back seat. Moonlight glinted
on his gun. It came down and pain exploded in him and he
continued to fall into a sea of silent darkness.

Chapter Twenty-one . . .

Early-morning sunlight struck painfully at his eyes, and Durell blinked and quickly shut them again. Fragments of memory drifted in his mind: the rocking, speeding car, Franz's big knees pressing on him as he lay on the back floor of the sedan, a lurching as they took a curve—and then he had blacked out again.

His head ached. His stomach jumped with nausea. There was a bitter taste in his mouth. He opened his eyes slightly until he could endure the brilliant light that shone in them. There was a strong, salty smell in the air, an odor of old timbers and decaying vegetation. Durell started to drift back into sleep, then forced himself up with a jolt as the full significance of the sunlight reached him. It was morning of the Fourth of July. He forced his eyes fully open and ignored the stabs of pain as he sat up.

At once a voice said. "Awake, Mr. Durell?"

John Padgett sat in a chair across the room. He was in a small chamber with a rough pine floor and a single window, through which the rays of the rising sun glared. There was an unpainted table, a kerosene stove, and a lamp hanging from a nail driven into the plank wall. Durell lay on a rough cot that smelled of age. When he sat up, nausea filled his mouth with saliva. Through the dirty window he glimpsed a beach overgrown with weeds, a few pilings in the muddy water, and a small white crab boat moored to a rickety plank dock.

"How do you feel, Mr. Durell?"

"Not good. Where is this place?"

"We are near Annapolis. You are tougher than I thought."

Durell swung his legs off the cot and sat up. It was warm in the barren room. Wasps hummed and bumped against the

139

slanted ceiling. Slowly his stomach settled and the pulse of pain in his head became tolerable. He said, "Where do we go from here?"

"Nowhere. We stay here."

"Do you know what you're doing, Padgett?"

"I am quite aware of everything."

"Then I don't understand why you're doing it."

"I suggested to you before that all matters are eventually leveled. Many things tip the scale so far in one direction that redress seems impossible. But only death is absolute, from which there can be no recall. In all other matters, one must strive, and sometimes one may succeed."

"Are you talking about your parents?"

Padgett nodded. "And my leg."

"You hold all that against society?"

"If I say yes, you will think me unbalanced. I am not mad. I know what I am doing. And I will be paid for my trouble, in money and security, in the pleasures of this one life we are all awarded, but in different measure."

"You don't care what happens when Cyclops comes down?"

"I need no lecture in humanitarianism. At the moment, I need information. Time is running out, Mr. Durell. Where are the papers you took from Calvin in Las Tiengas?"

Durell laughed. "I gave them to General McFee."

"You are lying," Padgett said quietly.

"Call him and see."

Padgett's face was gray. There were bandages on his right hand; he held his stick between his knees. In the silence, Durell heard the humming of the wasps and the lapping of the tide under the shack. The full orb of the sun was above the edge of the water now, dazzling, glaring, intolerably bright. Padgett spoke thoughtfully.

"McFee is convinced you are not to be trusted. I saw to that. And Swayney has no further use for you. Your bureau is convinced that my sister is a poor security risk and that you were influenced by her to betray your trust. What chance do you have, Durell? At four o'clock this afternoon, Cyclops goes up and comes down. If you survive the holocaust, will your vindication matter then?"

"What do you suggest?"

"You could come to South America with me. Co-operate now, relieve my mind of this last anxiety concerning Calvin's papers and my sister, and I will share the money involved. I know enough to build another Cyclops. There are international buyers for the plans I have."

Durell saw that Padgett was in sober earnest. But there was a dark, uneasy tension in the man as he sat there. Durell limped painfully to the window. The dawn sky looked daubed with blood. The window was nailed shut, but if he were alone, he could break the glass and escape that way. He looked at a hawk perched in a dead pine at the water's edge, and he looked at the molten sunlight on the bay. It all seemed strange and yet familiar, as if he saw it now for the first and the last time.

"You cannot escape," Padgett said quietly. "Franz is in the other room, and he will need little excuse to kill you. Where are Calvin's papers?"

"I told you. McFee has them."

"And Deirdre?"

"I won't tell you anything about her," Durell said.

Padgett took a small gun from his pocket and weighed it in his hand and looked at it. "Do you think anyone will miss you, Durell?"

"I don't matter very much," Durell said.

"You carry more weight than you think. But no one will find you in this Chesapeake mud, will they?"

Durell's head throbbed. "If you plan to shoot me, get it over with."

"Aren't you afraid to die?"

Durell was silent. Padgett sighed. He called for Franz, and when the big man appeared, Padgett limped across the room to Durell, and when he was within reach he suddenly slashed with the gun at Durell's face. Durell ducked and tried to reach for him, but Padgett swung and hit him in the face with the gun and Durell went down on hands and knees on the rough pine floor. When he shook his head, drops of bright blood spattered the dirty planks. His mind blurred. He started up and Franz kicked him in the ribs and he fell over.

Franz kicked him again. "Will you answer the questions?"

Durell got to his knees and lunged at Padgett, but Franz threw him back against the wall, caught a handful of his hair, and twisted his head cruelly to one side in a judo grip.

"Where is Deirdre?" Padgett shouted. "I must know!"

His voice seemed to come from a vast echoing distance

above Durell's head. Franz hit him again and the question was repeated. Durell told himself to get up and try for the door. He started to crawl for the doorway into the next room, and each move was a separate agony, and when he was almost there Franz quietly shut the door in his face.

"Where were you going to meet Deirdre?" Padgett yelled.

Durell rose swaying to his feet. He breathed pain. The room slipped out of focus. His pain lived in him and possessed him. He drew another breath and with his last strength threw a long right at Franz's face. He landed squarely. Franz crashed backward over a chair and slammed into the wall. Durell started to follow and saw Padgett lift his cane and chop down at his neck and he pitched forward into darkness again. . . .

He was on the same cot, in the same room. He absorbed pain with the darkness, his mind fleeing in confusion. His watch was real. The identity of the numbers on the dial was tangible. Eight o'clock. Morning or night?

Blindness. Was he blind?

Panic came with screaming mouth on the wings of a hurricane. He sat up and through the darkness he saw a faint slit of yellow where the door did not quite meet the sill. The cot squealed when he stood up.

Why was it dark?

He groped along the wall until he felt the casement of the window. His legs trembled; he was bathed in sweat. It was several more moments before he could go on, and while he rested he heard faint sounds from the other room and he felt reassured by the reality of those sounds. Somebody was there. He heard the muffled lapping of the tide around the pilings outside. The tide? Flooding or ebbing?

His fingers moved over the rough window frame and slid over the cool smoothness of glass. He could see nothing through it. Only total darkness.

Carefully he removed one of his shoes. Each gesture brought a new sea of pain that threatened to drown him. The effort to control his moves and maintain silence brought new outpourings of sweat. Then when he got the shoe off it fell from his fingers and thumped loudly on the floor.

He could have wept.

For an unendurable moment, nothing happened. He watched the slit of light under the doorway, and listened.

No one came. He bent and picked up the shoe again and swung it hard against the window. The glass shattered with an ear-splitting noise. Glass showered at him, slashing hands and arms as he reached for the window ledge. Franz yelled in the other room. But he had the catch now, and he swung the casement inward, then heaved himself up to go through.

There was a black, unyielding barrier beyond.

He lost his balance and fell heavily to the floor inside the room. Light bloomed behind him and then he saw there was a double wooden shutter on the window and it was closed and bolted from the outside. It explained the darkness, the fact that day had seemed to become night. He wanted to shout his relief at the reprieve of time.

Durell climbed slowly to his feet. Franz stood in the doorway, enormous, a looming silhouette against the light behind him.

"You son-of-a-bitch," Franz said softly.

Durell stood still as the giant cat-footed toward him.

When Franz was through with him, the tides of darkness moved back and forth while he fought to remain on the surface, awake and aware of himself. For a time he seemed to float high in space, and he heard Deirdre calling from the infinite starry darkness all around him. He tried to reach for her, and found he could not move. His hands and feet were tied to the cot.

He tried to get up. It was quiet in the room. He heard only the muted, inexorable tick of his watch. He wanted to look at it, but for a long time he was afraid to do so. Finally he twisted around to look at his wrist, tied to one of the legs of the cot, and he saw it was ten o'clock. His effort to see his watch seemed to loosen the knots that held his right arm, and he began to work at these knots patiently as the minutes passed away. . . .

He remembered a time when he was a boy. He was trapping in a swamp, and he had been careless when climbing over a wind drift. With no warning, several of the cypress logs gave way and plunged him into a deadfall. The heavy cypress boles pinned his legs, trapping him there in the isolated wilderness. The terror he had felt as a twelve-year-old boy came back sharply; he felt again the pain, the sounds of the bayou, the awful loneliness of the trapped. He remembered watching a coral snake move over the dead cypress knees; he remembered his frantic breathing, his efforts to lift the enormous weight from his legs. Panic held him. His teeth chattered. Sometimes he wept or shouted. Nobody came to help. The day waned, the sunlight died in the swamp. The insects came, humming, clicking, hungry. Once in the late night he saw distant lights and heard the halloos of searching men, like the voices of agonized ghosts. He had tried to shout, but it was as if a hand seized his throat and only a hoarse whisper came from him. Nobody came. Nobody would ever come. He would die unless he helped himself.

Finally he began scooping away the wet earth from under the logs, digging with his fingers until they bled. All sensation was gone from his legs. At dawn he was still digging at the hollow he had shaped under him. When at last he freed one leg, he could not move it, and he dragged at it with his hands, as if it were dead. Minutes later he got the other leg free and pulled himself away on his elbows. He had sobbed, because he thought his legs were paralyzed. But after a few minutes, just before he reached the *chenière*, pain came to them in fine tinglings and then in hot spasms of cramp that made him scream. He fainted when he finally dragged himself onto the road.

Later he remembered his grandfather on the hulk of the old side-wheeler, talking to him, saying things that made him feel proud. But those words and that time were gone now. . . .

Durell kept working on the knots that kept his right hand tied to the cot. He could make the line slip a little now, and he made a single effort, wrenching at the ropes. His skin tore on the back of his hand and blood oozed warmly over his fingers. The line slipped more easily because of the blood. He tried again. The rope slid almost to his knuckles and tightened again. He sweated. He could free himself no further. When he tried again, he knew his effort had grown more feeble.

He relaxed, gasping. Nobody came into the room. He twisted his head to look at his watch.

Eleven o'clock.

He thought of Deirdre and wondered where she was and why she had deserted him. He thought of Las Tiengas and the great, sprawling base in the hot desert, the unearthly machines and cranes and towers that lifted huge needle-shaped bulks to point toward the heavens. Up toward the stars! Someday it would happen; but not today. Today the wild power unleashed would fall back upon mankind, spreading destruction, death. He thought of John Padgett. What made a man feed on hate, relentless and unforgiving, shaking his fist at the silent, wheeling stars that had brought tragedy to his childhood? He understood Weederman, ex-Nazi, with no humility, no respite in defeat, setting former enemies at each other's throats, hoping for the world holocaust to avenge the fall of his own bloody tyranny. But for John Padgett to allow this catastrophe, to plan for it and strive and kill for it . . .

In the darkness of the room he heard the ping of his watch, the sound magnified by his taut senses; he visualized the tiny mainspring, the small hammer, the fine wheels and cogs and jeweled mechanism that marked the inexorable progress of life and death. He sensed the slow revolution of the earth on its axis in black space, turning seas and continents from shadow into light and into shadow again.

He worked at the knots on his wrist.

Now he was afraid to look at his watch again.

Much later, John Padgett came into the room, bringing yellow light that fell on Durell as he lay on the cot. Padgett limped to the cot and sat on a chair, his movements heavy. His bony shoulders and knees were all large, awkward angles.

"I am sorry we had to get rough, Durell. You are a stubborn man. For a time, I had the feeling I could not stop you." Padgett paused. "It's getting late now."

"I've been wondering," Durell said. "What happens if some of the fall-out covers this part of the coast? You go under along with everyone else."

"I will not be here. I am leaving soon for South America."

"For exile, you mean," Durell said. "And you have no pity for your victims?"

"They are merely statistics, and even as statistics, I hold hate and contempt for them. Man deserves a new Stone Age." Padgett's voice was harsh. "I had great promise once. I was a child prodigy, a mathematical wizard. It was like carrying an electronic computer around in my head. But because my father and mother died penniless, nothing much came of it. I hated my torn and crippled leg, the poverty, the struggle, the times I was put on display at various universities and exhibited as if I were a freak. Do you understand? But Cyclops will make it all even."

"Did you work on the scheme with Weederman?"

"Of course. We understood each other. But I kept what I knew to myself. He would have preferred blueprints, naturally, and schematic diagrams. I gave him nothing."

"You killed him," Durell said.

"He became obsessed with the thought that I was not keeping my part of the bargain. He upbraided me for leaving the fold, knowing my early record, knowing how I had joined various organizations under Calvin's name. I would not tolerate him or his words. He repelled me. What I did was solely for myself, do you understand?"

"No," Durell said.

"He had no reason to kill Calvin," Padgett said.

"So you avenged him?"

"Call it that. He was interfering with me."

"And now you insist on finishing what you've started?"

"I must."

Durell said, "I'm sorry for you, John. Do you know that?"

"Sorry?" Padgett's voice sharpened. "I did not come in here for your maudlin sympathy. What have you got to be smug about, as you are?"

"I'm not smug. I'm afraid. I've never been so afraid before. And yet I'm sorry for you."

Padgett was suddenly in a deep rage. He lurched up from the chair, knocking it over with a crash, and turned as if to leave the room. Then he limped back, cane in hand, and towered enormously over the cot. Durell could not move. Reaching down, Padgett covered Durell's mouth with a trembling hand, fingers digging lightly, then with cruel strength into Durell's flesh. Abruptly he slapped Durell. Durell made no sound. Padgett lifted the cane and hit his body again and again, and the worst of it for Durell was that it was all done in silence except for the shock and sound of the blows. It was a silence that screamed of perverted hatreds.

When Padgett stepped back, gasping, Durell still had not made a sound.

"Damn you," the man whispered, and left the room.

Chapter Twenty-two . . .

His watch had stopped. He could not remember when he
had wound it last, and now it was silent, marking the hour
of noon. Time and space held him in sluggish suspension, in
which the lightning of pain slowly grew dim.

Because of the shuttered window, the room was still dark
when he began working again at the ropes on his wrist. The
blood from his torn skin had clotted on the line, and his
first efforts tore the clots loose with a single shriek of pain.
Sweating, he felt fresh blood ooze from the back of his
hand. But now the rope slid easily over the lubrication provided by the wound. On the third try, the rope slid over one
knuckle and the widest part of his twisted palm.

And suddenly his hand was free.

He lay still. A pattering sound filled the darkness, and
he could not identify it. Then he knew it was rain. The rain
became a sudden downpour, and its thunder and beat provided a cover for his next moves. His fingers were stiff,
hampered by pain. He tore at the stubborn braids with his
teeth until he had to stop and rest. He could hear nothing
above the rattle and beat of summer rain on the roof. A leak
began in the opposite corner of the room.

Now both hands were free. But he was shaking and spent
when he finally sat up and swung his legs off the cot and
tried to stand.

His legs collapsed. They would not support him. He
pulled himself up and massaged them. The cot creaked with
his movements. A chair thumped suddenly in the next room
and Durell was still, listening to the guttural sound of Franz's
voice, hating it with every fiber of his being. After another
moment, he tried to stand again.

This time he succeeded, but he swayed like a drunken

147

man. He wanted to let it all go. He wanted to stop punishing himself, to sleep and forget. But he could not sleep and he could not forget.

There was a cunning in him like that of an animal, and his thoughts did not move in fully rational channels. Breathing quietly, he tried to sense through the darkness the position of chairs and table. When he shuffled forward, he immediately felt the wooden chair that John Padgett had overturned. He knew there was no hope beyond the door where Franz waited. Yet his mind pursued one path, surely and directly.

He remembered the oil lantern hanging on the wall.

He went for it slowly, testing the floor so it would not creak with his weight. Once he stood frozen as he heard another spate of talk from beyond the door. The rain drummed hard on the roof. Thunder muttered, and he shivered in the clammy air that filled the room. Finally he reached the opposite wall and found the oil lantern hanging from its nail, as he had remembered it.

Briefly, as he held it by the wire handle, he suffered a terrible fear that the oil reservoir was empty. But when he shook it, he heard the soft splash of fuel inside.

Now he worked faster, at the window, feeling for the glass he had smashed earlier. His fingers were clumsy at the job of unscrewing the oil cap, and then, reaching through the broken window, he splashed the oil carefully on the wooden shutter that barred him from freedom. There was not much oil. He saved some to form a pool on the window sill, and then he put down the lantern and searched his clothing for a match.

He had no match.

He stood still in dark defeat. His mind refused to function further. He could not move. Thunder rolled and the rain came down with new intensity. He heard Franz talking again. At last he turned and moved back to the wall where he had found the lantern. He could see nothing. He groped on the shelf, fumbled around the contours of several cans, a glass bottle, more cans. His fingers closed around a box of wooden matches.

Back at the window, the smell of spilled kerosene stung his nostrils. His hands shook as he struck a match and watched it sputter and burst into flame like a tiny bomb.

The kerosene caught with a hiss and crackle and the room

suddenly glowed with the fire that leaped up the wooden shutter. Durell stepped back. Smoke curled and lifted through the room. The hungry flames ate at the tinder-dry sill and the shutter that barred his way. The smoke made his eyes smart. He wondered how long it would be before Franz noticed the smoke, and he picked up the wooden chair John Padgett had used and held it ready in his hands.

An impatience seized him as he watched the growing flames, but he waited until the last possible moment. When he heard Franz's sudden shout of alarm as the smoke finally reached the other room, Durell smashed the chair with all his strength against the burning barrier. The chair shattered in his grip. From behind him came another shout, and then the sound of bolts being withdrawn from the door. Durell slammed the chair remnants against the shutter again. This time the burning wood burst open and fell in flaming brands inside and out of the room. The heat seared Durell's face as the fire was blown inward. Smoke blinded him.

"Durell! Stay where you are!"

It was Franz, roaring in exasperation. Durell hurled the burning, broken chair at the doorway and, without waiting to see the result, gathered himself and dived headlong through the burning window.

Broken glass ripped at his arms and hands and then he was through, rolling over and over in the thick marsh grass outside, stumbling and splashing through ankle-deep salt water. He stood up, drawing in great breaths of cool, fresh air. The rain beat heavily on his head. He saw that the bay and the shore all around him were bathed in the gray, rain-swept light of early afternoon.

He ran. Someone shouted, and he looked back and saw the whole side of the shack in flames. It was a tumbledown affair on stilts at the water's edge. There was a small inlet where the crab boat was moored, and a dirt road that curved through a wilderness of swamp and scrub woods. The heavy foliage drooped forlornly in the pounding rain. To the south the beach was open, a wide vista of salt-water flats; northward, the swamp was a thickly matted growth that crowded to the water's edge.

Franz and John Padgett came out of the cabin. Both were armed. They looked his way and Franz fired and Durell threw himself flat, picked himself up, ran for the cover of the swamp. The rain slashed coldly at his face. Looking back, he saw Franz coming fast, too fast, head lowered, gun ready. John Padgett limped along to the rear. Durell sprinted for the protective screen of a hazelnut bush. A bullet whined past his head, another slapped angrily into the ground inches away. Gasping, Durell flung himself forward toward some cedars. Then for the space of several racking breaths he could not move.

The rain hissed all around him. In every direction there was nothing but wilderness, no house to which he could run for help. The gray daylight filled him with incalculable dismay. He ached in every bone and muscle. Through the wet leaves he saw that Franz had halted and was talking to John Padgett, who leaned on his cane. Both men faced him, but they could not see him until he chose to move.

He sprawled as he was and did not stir.

The two men were quarreling.

As he watched, he heard their angry voices, bitter with recrimination, rise and fall above the sound of the rain. The swamp made a green wet curtain all around him. The daylight seemed brighter and stronger. Then he saw John Padgett lift his cane and strike at the other man. Franz took the blow on his face and struck back with a massive fist, just once. Padgett fell, his crippled leg twisted under him. Franz stood over him, hulking, powerful, shouting something. Then the giant's head jerked up and he started purposefully toward the clump of cedars and brush where Durell was hidden.

Panic picked him up and flung him through the swamp. A gun cracked. As he ran, the wind whistling in his throat, he thought the swamp was endless. He glimpsed the gray Chesapeake, dimpled by the rain. His thoughts blurred. Then he found a trail and jogged along, gasping. Franz was behind him. A hawk screamed thinly in the overcast and he saw its dim shape floating above the trees. The rain was only a drizzle. The road was endless. It went nowhere. His heart hammered, his throat was raw.

He halted. He could go no farther.

He was through running.

He saw that Franz had halted, too, and for the space of a few breaths they stared at each other. And Durell thought of Lew Osbourn and Sidonie and the house in Alexandria;

he thought of Calvin Padgett, dead in a desert barn; of Feener, dead in the bayous.

Anger rose in him. He felt no fear. He pushed fear away from him.

"Durell!" Franz called.

A bird twittered in the leafy branches overhead.

The voice echoed. "Come, Durell. We will go back."

Durell walked toward him. The dirt road was puddled and muddy. A thin glimmer of watery sunshine slanted down through the swamp. Franz kept the gun pointed at him. He stood hulking, ominous, in the fine rain. Durell was within jumping distance of the gun. Not now. Not yet. His deep anger was linked with his decision not to run any more. This was the enemy.

He no longer felt tired.

"Stop," Franz said thickly. "This is as far as you go. You held us up long enough."

"Did you kill John Padgett?"

"I do not know. Shut up. Start walking ahead of me."

Durell walked heavily through the mud on the path. "It's too late for you to get away from Cyclops now, Franz. You're caught in it along with all the rest of us."

"Shut up!" Franz yelled. "Walk!"

Sweat mingled with the rain on the giant's face. His wide mouth shook. They entered a small leafy clearing, and a thin wind came with the end of the rain and it rustled and whispered through the foliage and Durell felt its summer warmth against his face. Franz looked ill. There was something wrong with him. Durell felt a quick lift of strength as he recognized what it was. Franz was afraid. His thrust about the danger from Cyclops had gone home.

Durell jumped for him then. There was eight feet between them, and he knew he couldn't hope to make it. He heard the gun roar and saw the convulsive spasm on Franz's face and something hit his left shoulder like the flat of a board swung with incredible strength. The impact drove him twisting down; and he landed on his hands and knees. He felt no pain, but time slowed until everything could be seen in careful, minute detail, and one of the things he saw was that Franz had not moved. And he saw that as Franz stood there, gun in hand, legs spread a little in the soft, wet mud, Franz was going to fire again. Durell came up with a stone in his hand and threw it, all in one movement as he twisted aside.

The stone hit Franz in the face and the man screamed. The gun crashed again, but the bullet went into the gray sky, and a few leaves came flickering down after its passage and a crow cawed in fright. Durell got his legs under him and lunged forward again.

There was blood on Franz's face and there was something wrong with his right eye, where the stone had hit him. Durell swung at the gun and knocked it aside and drove Franz back with his charge. Franz took his rush on one hip and slammed against a young swamp maple, but the gun was jolted from his hand and spun to the ground. Instinctively Franz dropped to reach for it and Durell chopped at his thick neck with all the strength left in him, and chopped again. Franz fell to his knees with his eyes glazed, mouth open, face twisted by surprise.

Durell hit him again and tried to use his left, but he had no control over his left arm. It hung uselessly, without pain or feeling in it. Blood welled from his left shoulder, where the bullet had gone in, and dripped from his fingers. Then Franz came up with a shout and slammed into Durell and drove him across the clearing, across the dirt road, and into the swamp beyond. Durell broke free and rolled over in the muddy water, and Franz, on his knees, hit him with a fist like a hammer.

The gun was forgotten. Neither had any use for it. It would not have provided a satisfactory victory for either man. Only flesh against flesh, bone against bone, would answer the hatred between them. Durell tried to rise but his left hand went out from under him and his face hit the swampy water and he rolled aside. Panic spurted in him. Franz stood over him. Before he could escape, Franz kicked him and then jumped as if to land on him with his knees, but Durell kicked upward and Franz screamed and doubled up.

Slowly Durell climbed to his feet. Pain went through him in dark waves. He looked at Franz and saw the hatred in him and he looked for the gun. He couldn't find it. Franz got up, his mouth open, and came at him with a splashing rush. Durell went down under his weight, dragged deep into the mire. The tall reeds closed over him. Franz pushed his head under the surface. Durell rolled with the other's weight, held his breath, and arched convulsively. Franz slid aside and Durell was on top.

There was a roaring in his ears and a dimness all around

him. His strength ran out with the slow drip of blood from his wounded shoulder. The water was stained a bright red. He felt Franz's weakened movements, his last effort to break free. The man's face came up, mouth straining for air, and Durell hit him and he went under again. The wind swayed the tall marsh reeds. Somewhere a squirrel scolded.

Durell stood up. He swayed, spread-legged. He was shaking, and his teeth chattered. He pulled free of the clinging ooze and reached down for Franz's collar and hauled the man's head out of the water. Something came in a quick gush over Franz's lips. Stumbling, Durell fought his way back to the dirt road, dragging the unconscious man with him. Once out of the water, he let Franz sprawl as he was and searched about until he found the gun. When he picked it up, he saw the sun shining in bright shafts of gold through the swamp trees.

Franz was breathing again. Franz sat up. He looked at the gun in Durell's hand. And Durell felt an overpowering impulse to squeeze the trigger.

"Get up," he gasped.

Franz stood up.

"Now we'll go back," Durell said.

There was a smell of smoke and charred, wet wood when they returned to the shack. The tumbledown structure had not burned completely. Apparently the rain had quenched the fire before more than half of it was consumed by the flames.

John Padgett still sprawled on the beach where Franz had hit him. Durell needed only one look at him. The man was dead. Franz made a soft sound and stood a little aside, head sunk in his massive shoulders. Now and then he looked apprehensively at the sky.

"You hit him too hard," Durell said.

"It makes no difference," Franz said dully. "Maybe he is the lucky one."

"It may not be too late."

"Our plane has already left. He waited too long. I argued and argued with him. But he waited because of you. And because he was uncertain about his sister."

Durell gestured with the gun. "Let's go inside."

Franz moved with sodden steps. In the other room of the shack, which Durell had not seen before, were two leather suitcases and a diplomat's dispatch case. Durell broke open the case and looked quickly through the neatly clipped folders of blueprints and diagrams and mathematical formulae. It was Cyclops, the new star in the heavens, neatly documented and diagramed for reproduction elsewhere in the world.

"Where is the car we came in?" Durell asked.

"Not far. In the bushes near the highway."

Durell took the dispatch case with him when they left the shack. The car was not difficult to find. Durell paused. "What time is it?"

Franz had a watch.

"It is two o'clock," he said.

"Let's get to a telephone."

Chapter Twenty-three . . .

Dickinson McFee's office at 20 Annapolis Street was crowded, thick with smoke, disturbed by the press of people who came and went. Durell sat in a leather armchair in the corner. A doctor worked over his face. He was stripped to the waist, and white bandages covered the wound in his shoulder. He listened to the incessant ringing of the telephones, the crisp orders McFee handed out, the quick patter of feet, the heavy breathing of the doctor. The antiseptic burned, stung, soothed. Someone put a cigarette in his mouth and he dragged at it gratefully.

Hazel was tearful. "Oh, Sam. Are you all right?"

McFee answered for him, shortly. "He'll live."

"But he ought to be in a hospital!"

"We'll ship him there soon."

"He ought to be there this *minute!*"

"Hazel, get out of here."

Telephones jangled. Swayney came in, looked helpless, went out. Art Greenwald stood by soberly. Durell had talked steadily for an hour, after the police car had picked him up at the service station on the highway to Washington. He smoked his cigarette. He let the doctor work on him. Nobody had mentioned Deirdre's name.

Padgett's dispatch case was on McFee's desk. Franz was being questioned in one of the rooms upstairs. Franz had collapsed completely with his fear of Cyclops. Durell felt as if he were suspended in a glimmering drop of liquid, waiting for that drop to fall and burst and destroy him.

McFee came over. "This place is a madhouse. Sam, can you hear me?"

Durell nodded. "Where is Cyclops?"

McFee nodded toward the window and the dark sky.

155

Durell realized with a shock that it was night. "Up there somewhere, Sam. The telescopes are on her."

"Then Cyclops is *orbiting?*"

"Right on schedule."

"Then Calvin Padgett was wrong. I was wrong. I—"

"Take it easy. The boy's figures were right. Those you left on my desk, I mean. You've had a hard time, Sam, and I'm afraid I didn't make it any easier for you. Lucky I had sense enough to have the equations run through a calculator at the Pentagon. After that, it was a matter of calling Las Tiengas and taking the hex out of the brain that John Padgett put into it. Cyclops was launched on schedule, but the fact that she's orbiting now is only due to you. Considering the state of the world, the State Department lads now have a sure position of strength from which to talk for us, for a change."

Durell nodded. He asked about his grandfather. Jonathan was in New Orleans, at a fine hotel, having the time of his life. Compliments of the FBI.

He felt himself going out on a deep tide of darkness then. He struggled back to where he could see Dickinson McFee once more.

"The girl," he said. "Deirdre Padgett. Where is she?"

McFee was silent.

Durell struggled up. "Go on. Tell me."

The doctor pushed him back into the chair. "Sit down, pal. I've got work to do."

McFee said gently, "We don't know, Sam. We've looked everywhere. We're still looking. But it doesn't seem good."

"You've got to find her!"

"We'll try, Sam. We'll do our best."

He slept the clock around in the Naval Hospital room, and it was late afternoon again when he awoke. He felt better. His head was clear. There was little or no pain. There was a nurse in the room, cool, efficient, and he asked her for his clothes. When she refused, Durell got out of bed and the nurse called the floor intern, the intern called the resident physician, the resident came hurrying in to speak to Durell. By that time Durell was dressed and sitting on the edge of his bed, using the telephone.

He called Hazel. "Have they found Deirdre yet?"

"Oh, Sam, I don't think so."

"Get me Swayney."

To Swayney: "Where is the girl?"

"Sam, look, I'm sorry for everything—"

"You were doing your job and I don't want apologies, Burritt. All I want is the girl."

"We can't find her, Sam . . . Sam?"

"Get me Dickinson McFee."

To McFee: "Padgett didn't have her, Franz didn't have her, you don't have her. Where in hell is she?"

"We don't know, Sam."

"She didn't just run away for the hell of it!"

"Are you sure of that, Sam?"

"What are you talking about?"

"Didn't you quarrel with her, or something like that?" Durell thought about it. "I'm not certain."

"Look, as long as you're up and about, you ought to give Sidonie Osbourn a ring. She's been trying to reach you by telephone, but the hospital people had orders to let you sleep. Call her, Sam."

"Sidonie? I'll do better than that. I'll go see her."

The nurse, intern, and resident objected. Durell brushed past them and went out of the hospital and hailed a cab and had himself driven to Alexandria.

The curving street looked serene and peaceful in the evening light. There had been no publicity attached to Cyclops. Not yet. Nobody was out on the sidewalk looking at the sky except two small boys flying kites. Durell paid the cab driver and slowly went up the walk to the small, comfortable house. He felt awkward in the tight bandages that restricted his left arm. He felt awkward for the first moment when Sidonie Osbourn opened the door, and after that it was all right.

"Come in, Sam. Are you sure you ought to be up and around so soon?"

He kissed her cheek. "I heard you wanted to talk to me. Are the girls O.K.?"

"They're fine."

"Are you working for Dickinson McFee yet?"

"I start tomorrow."

"Sid . . ."

"You're just in time for dinner. Come into the kitchen. The girls are eating out at a neighbor's."

"I'm not hungry," Durell said. "I just—"

"Don't ever say that to a Frenchwoman!" she mocked him.

She tugged at his arm. "And don't look so forlorn. It's all right." Then she sobered. "Truly, Sam. I told you how it was with Lew and me. It's all right. Or at least, I know it couldn't have been avoided. Lew was doing his job."

The kitchen was warm and comfortable. He watched Sidonie move about, setting the table, checking the food in the oven. She looked fresh and clean and wonderful. He felt an ache deep inside him, a vast loneliness. He wanted to talk to her about Deirdre, but he couldn't. They talked about everything else.

Finally, over coffee, Sidonie said quietly, "Sam, do you feel sorry for me?"

"I think you're fine and brave. No, I don't feel sorry for you now."

"Do you still feel you can travel faster and farther alone? Because your job is dangerous, you should have no ties to anyone?"

"I don't know," he said. "But I know now that you and Lew did the right thing. I want some of it for myself, now."

"Then you've changed your mind," she said.

"I found a girl. But I've lost her again."

"Have you looked everywhere for her?"

"I've had the whole damned section looking—" He broke off, staring at her. "What do you know about Deirdre?"

"She was here. Right here. You told her about Lew and me, in the bayou, so she came to me. She told me about that night. And what Swayney said. It hasn't been easy for her. She said you saved her from a lonely, empty life. And she said she'd be waiting for you."

"Where is she?" Durell was on his feet. "Tell me."

Sidonie smiled. "She's waiting in your apartment. The one place no one thought to look. Now kiss me good night and get on your horse and go."

He ran up the stairs, down the hall, to the doorway. The door was not locked. He stood in the entrance and she was there. He looked at her, curled up on his favorite leather chair. The lamp made her red hair a bright glow. She wore a soft dress of cream and gold and she looked different and he did not know what it was that was different about her, at first; and then he realized that he saw her now in composure, without fear, scrubbed and clean and rested, not as she had been in the bayou or before that or afterward. And the way she looked squeezed something inside him and he felt suddenly as if she were a stranger and all his thoughts about her had been only dangerous dreams.

"So here you are," he said banally.

"Hello, Sam."

"You . . . What happened to you?"

"Come in. Close the door, Sam. I didn't know where else to go, so I came here. I've been here ever since that last bad night." She paused. "That was the night I thought they had killed you. After McFee's, I mean. Then I remembered you mentioned Sidonie Osbourn, so I called her and she told me what you had done. So I've just been waiting here for you to come home."

"I've been worried sick."

"I'm sorry."

"Half out of my mind."

"I'm glad."

Her eyes were mischievous. He came into the room and looked down at her. "What happened to you outside of McFee's?"

"I saw Franz on the street," she said. "I was stunned. I guessed he had been watching McFee's for you to show up. But then he started away and I jumped out of the car to follow him and then I lost him. I'd have taken the car, only I don't know how to drive. When I got back there were the police and a big crowd outside McFee's house and I knew it had gone all wrong for you. I thought you were arrested. Or killed. I didn't know what to do. So I called Sidonie and went there. Then I came here. And waited. And died a thousand times and shed an ocean of tears. Because I love you, Sam."

Now her eyes were grave. She stood up and went to the window. "Sidonie told me all about you. How you always thought it was foolish to get involved with someone you loved, because of your job and all the things that might happen."

"So?"

She turned to face him. "It's up to you. If you want me to go, I'll go."

"Could you?"

"No," she said. "Yes. I don't know. I don't think so. Oh, I don't know what I'm trying to say."

Suddenly as they stood by the window she began to shake

and then she was in his arms. He told her to look out at the evening sky. The first stars were beginning to shine.

"It's all over now," he said. "It's all right."

"Is it?" She stared at the darkening sky. "Cyclops is up there, somewhere. Over our heads. It will always be there, from now on."

"Like the conscience of humanity," Durell said quietly.

"You . . . Sam?"

Her eyes questioned him. He smiled. He kissed her.

"Come closer," he said.

"Sam?"

"I'll never let you go," he said.